BEST BOOKS
倍斯特出版事業有限公司
Best Publishing Ltd.

U0057214

心智圖輕鬆學

Fun Email 寫作好 easy

擁有 **12** 主題
×
3 大情境

你要的 email 寫作
就是這本

創意思考
/
迅速破題
/
靈活運用

公關─活動時間是？
客服─小姐取貨囉？
廠商─約個交貨期？
採購─這多少錢哩？
業務─咱們合作吧？
求職─我面試過了？
留學─哪裏有住宿？
學校─推薦信O，嗎？
網購─貨物配送日？
投訴─新買有問題？
訂房─房間訂完沒？
旅行─簽證過了嗎？

陳 瑾珮

有了本書 | 寫 email 真是好靈活・好 easy

作者序

　　面對全球化、國際化的浪潮，英文不再只是學校的一門科目，而是求學、求職的必備技能，且已漸漸超越學歷，成為企業徵人、考核升遷的重要依據。但在我教授國高中英文和成人美語十多年的教學生涯中，我看到太多人遭遇「背萬千字，卻寫不出一段書信」的窘境。

　　許多人面對白紙或電腦發呆，好像知道要寫什麼，卻思緒雜亂或害怕寫錯，遲遲無法下筆或打字，寫作成了最終極的挑戰。

　　為了幫助學生克服恐懼，寫出適合各種情境的E-mail，我使用過多種寫作訓練教材。但常感嘆坊間E-mail書信書籍多半針對每個主題「只給予一篇範文」和多個「同義代換句」，內容看似多元豐富，但實際能套用「同主題，但不同需求或重點」的應用度極低。

　　於是我採取新的途徑來幫助讀者，針對不同「主題」提供「心智圖」組織訊息內容，設計E-mail各段架構、套用句型、主題單字及代換段落，讓讀者可以針對不同的對象，套用合適的段落，讓完成的E-mail書信更貼近「量身訂做」，而非「抄寫範文」。

　　我在這本書中收錄常見的商務與生活情境，涵蓋12項E-mail核心主題，每項主題再細分為3個情境，設計了最具代表性的中英對照範例，以商務書信的文體格式，為職場人士或即將踏入職場的學子提供各種情境需求的範文，幫助讀者E-mail寫作快速又精準！

　　這本書除了是「辦公室E-mail的工具書」，也能幫助讀者提升英文程度—對於高中或大專院校的使用者來說，本書可協助準備升學考試中翻英、文法句型、單字片語及應用文寫作；對於上班族來說，也是自我英語進修，精進各類型英語檢定考試的寶典！

Jennifer 陳瑾珮

編者序

　　E-mail是現在非常方便的一種聯絡方式，無論相隔多遠，只要電腦或是智慧型手機，就能透過網路發送E-mail。但是用英文寫E-mail對許多人說，確實是一件頭痛的事。因為不知道該如何開始，那麼英文書信的撰寫，應該注意哪些地方呢?

　　傳統教導E-mail寫作，通常會請學生先想好要寫幾個段落，每一個段落訂出一個主題後，再想topic sentence，然後再……，許多人到這一步已經是一個頭兩個大了，本書提供讀者運用mind mapping，將新舊概念加以整合，期待用一種創新、簡單又有效率的方式去學習E-mai寫作的方法與技巧。讓讀者們不再對使用E-mai寫作感到困擾，善用心智圖法，你就能快速建立屬於自己的字彙資料庫。

倍斯特編輯部

目錄

Unit 1

旅行

情境一
套裝行程

情境二
簽證過了嗎

情境三
旅客登機資訊確認

情境一　套裝行程

心智圖解說

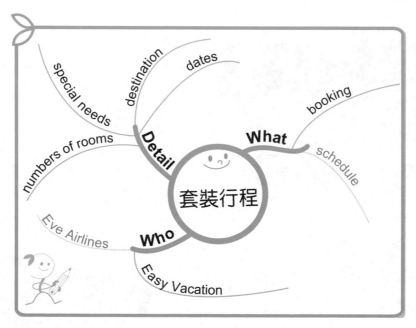

寫作技巧錦囊

Who is the thank-you note for?　這封感謝函是要給誰？
→ Easy Vacation

What can the travel agency help you with?　旅行社能協助你什麼？
→ booking

Details of your request / trip　特殊要求／旅行的細節
→ destination; dates; requirements; numbers of rooms; special needs

單字片語搶先看

1. **To Whom It May Concern** 敬啟者 （信件開頭稱謂語）
2. **flight** *n.[C]* 班機
   - Ben caught the first flight out of Washington this morning for Tokyo.
     Ben搭乘今早最早一班離開華盛頓的班機前往日本。

3. **depart** *vi.* 離開；出境 ⟷ arrive
   - Dan departed from Taipei for Shanghai last Friday on business.
     Dan上週五搭機從台北去上海出差。
     詞類變化：departure *n.[C, U]* 離開；出發
     句型：depart from 從……離開 depart for 前往……

4. **prefer** *vt.* 偏愛
   - Most people nowadays prefer tablets to laptops.
     現代人大多偏愛平板電腦勝過傳統筆電。

5. **airlines** *n. plural* 航空公司
   - China Airlines has been providing direct flights across the Strait in the past three years.
     華航過去這三年來提供兩岸直航的服務。

6. **return ticket** 來回票 ⟷ one-way ticket
   - Make sure you book return tickets instead of one-way tickets on the website.
     要確定你在網站上訂的是來回票而不是單程票。

7. **metro** *n.[C]* 地下鐵
   - This hotel is within walking distance to the nearest metro station.
     這家旅館步行即可抵達距離最近的捷運站。

8. **prompt** *adj.* 迅速的 *(= rapid, quick)*
   - Thank you for your prompt reply to my inquiry.
     謝謝您迅速回覆我的問題。

英文範例

【★可替換其他需求】

對象：旅行社

To Whom It May Concern, — 對象

My husband and I are interested in your special summer offers. We would like you to help book flights and hotels for our family trip to Tokyo. We plan to depart from Kaohsiung on Aug. 8th and return on Aug. 13th. ★ Regarding the return tickets, we prefer China Airlines. As for accommodation, we'd like to stay at a — 協助事項 five star hotel with easy access to the metro. Since we'll bring our five-year-old son and my two parents with us, we need to book two rooms, one suite and one double. — 特殊要求

Thank you for your prompt attention to the above and I look forward to receiving your email.

Kind regards,

Jasmine Lu

段落大意

主要需求	開場告知旅程的目的地，以及出發和回程時間。
細節	詳述對旅館、機票的需求細節。
敬請回覆	請對方提供相關旅遊資訊供你選擇。
信尾	客套語 ＋ 署名。

中文翻譯

敬啟者：

我先生和我對你們的夏日優惠方案很感興趣。我們想請您幫忙訂購我們到東京家族旅行的機加酒行程。我們計畫八月八日從高雄出發，八月十三日回台。

我們偏好訂購華航的來回機票。關於住宿的部分，我門希望住在離捷運站近的五星級旅館。因為我們會帶五歲的兒子和我的父母一同出遊，所以我們需要訂兩個房間——一間套房和一間雙人房。

謝謝您迅速為我們處理以上事宜，期待收到您的電郵回覆。

親切的問候，

Jasmine 盧　敬上

換個對象寫寫看

飯店地點軟／硬體的需求

- We'd like to stay at a centrally-located hotels which is located near major attractions, or at least with easy access to public transportations. We prefer hotels that run shuttles to and from popular sightseeing destinations, or are possible to get to places on foot. Besides, my parents are both over 75 and disabled, so we are looking for hotels which are wheelchair accessible with widened doorways. It's best to have internet connection, sauna, and Jacuzzi.
  我們想要找位於樞紐地帶，且鄰近主要旅遊景點的旅館，至少大眾交通工具要很方便。我們偏愛提供接駁車來往熱門觀光景點，或可以步行抵達景點的旅館。此外我的父母年紀都超過75歲且行動不便，所以我們在找輪椅可以通行且門前走道較寬敞的旅館。最好提供上網、蒸汽浴和按摩浴缸等設施。

機票的需求

- We are looking for the cheapest flight deals. Direct flights are desirable, but long stopovers or transit flights *are not a problem.*
  我們在找最便宜的機票。直達班機當然最好，但長時間的中途停留或轉機的航班也沒問題。

其他詢問旅遊資訊的萬用語

- Would you please send us a list of suggested hotels with prices?
  你能寄給我們您所推薦的旅館清單，並附上住房價格嗎？
- We would very much appreciate it if you can send us recommended tour packages and detailed itinerary.
  若您可以提供您推薦的旅遊行程和詳細行程表，我們將非常感激。
- We will be glad to receive your suggested hotel and flight packages.
  我們會很高興，收到您推薦的機酒套裝行程。
- We would find it most helpful if you can compare flight fares and hotel rates and fax us the details.
  若您能比較機票費用和旅館住房房價，並將資料傳真給我們，那將幫我們一個大忙。

句型解說在這裡

句型1

as for / regarding ＋ N　　至於、關於⋯⋯

☞ Regarding / As for you application, we'll proceed it as soon as possible.
關於你的申請案，我們會盡速處理。

延伸觀念

concerning
with regard to　＋ N　　關於⋯⋯
Relating to
about

☞ I'm calling concerning / with regard to / regarding to / about my application to the position.
我來電了解我求職應徵的事。

句型2

since ＋ S ＋ V　　既然⋯⋯

☞ Since you have nothing to do tomorrow, why don't we see a movie together?
既然你明天沒事，我們何不一起去看電影？

延伸句型

自從⋯⋯

since⋯⋯

☞ I haven't heard from you since I moved to Japan.
自從我搬到日本後，就再也沒聽到你的消息了。

練習時間試試看

預訂去韓國首爾五天四夜的機票和酒店

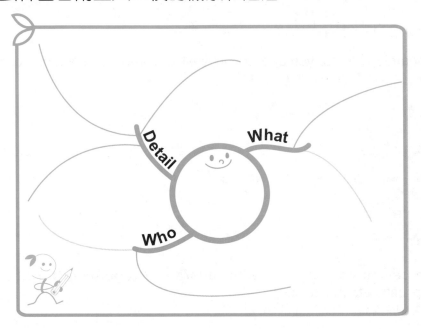

 Who are you writing to? 要寫給誰？

 What can the travel agency help you with? 旅行社能協助你處理什麼？

 Details of your request / trip 特殊要求／旅行的細節

練習範例分享

To Whom It May Concern,

My wife and I would like you to help book flights and

hotels for our family trip to Seoul. We plan to depart from

Taipei on Dec. 5th and return on Dec. 9th.

Since we're heading for the most popular ski resort,

The Ski Paradise, we'd like to book a room for 2 adults

and 2 children directly inside the resort villa for four

nights. We also need you to sign up the local ski

courses for my two kids.

Please forward me the details of the flight and hotel

packages.

Thank you for your prompt attention to the above and I

look forward to hearing from you soon.

Regards,

Julie Fan

對象

協助事項

特殊要求

敬啟者：

我太太和我想請您幫我們全家訂購韓國首爾之行機加酒行程。我們計畫12月5日從台北出發，12月9日回台。

因為我們要去當地最熱門的滑雪聖地——滑雪天堂，我們想要直接在滑雪度假村內訂一房（兩大兩小）過四個晚上。我們也要請您協助幫兩個孩子報名當地滑雪課程。

請提供機票和訂房資料。

謝謝您迅速為我們處理以上事宜，我期待盡快收到您的回覆。
Julie 范　敬上

情境二 簽證過了嗎

心智圖解說

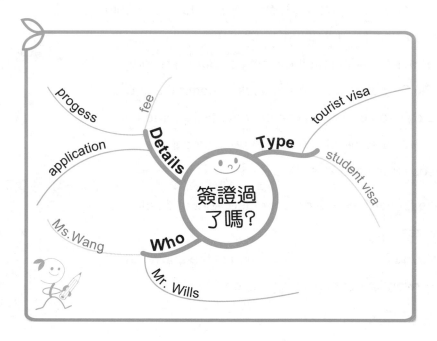

progess
fee
tourist visa
Details
Type
student visa
application
簽證過了嗎？
Ms.Wang
Who
Mr. Wills

寫作技巧錦囊

Step 1   **Who** are you writing to?   寫給誰？
→ Mr. Wills

Step 2   **What** type of visa are you applying for?   你要申請什麼樣的簽證？
→ tourist visa

Step 3   **Details** of Visa Application   簽證申請書的細節
→ application; progress

單字片語搶先看

1. status *n.[C]* 狀態 *(= condition, position, situation)*
    - What's your marital status? Are you married or not?
    你的婚姻狀態為何？你結婚或未婚？

2. lodge *vi. vt.* 暫住；提出 *(= submit, hand in)*
    - He lodged an appeal with the High Court.
    他向高等法院提出上訴。

3. reference *n.[C]* 參考
    - These students checked out a lot of reference books for their research.
    這些學生借閱了很多參考書籍做研究。

4. process *vt.* 處理
    - Are you experienced in using the up-dated word-processing software?
    你很熟悉如何操作這個更新版文書處理軟體嗎？

5. approximately *adv.* 大約 *(= about, close to)*
    - Commuting to and from work takes me approximately one and half hours every day.
    我每天工作通勤時間大約用掉一個半小時。

6. issue *vt. vi.* 核發；流出 *(= grant, approve of)*
    - The US State department issues millions of passports each year.
    美國政府每年核發數百萬的護照。

7. progress *n.[U]* 進度
    - Please keep me posted on the progress of the event.
    請隨時告知我這起事件的最新發展。

英文範例

【★可替換不同簽證情況】

> 詢問旅遊代辦業者你所申請的韓國旅行簽證核發了沒

Dear Mr. Wills,

對象

★ I'm writing this letter to ask about the status of my tourist visa application to Canada, which was lodged on Dec. 15. My application reference number is Z00325.

申請書相關

I learned from your website that visa processing time is approximately 7 to 10 working days. It's been two weeks since I submitted my application, and I'd like to know whether my visa has been issued, or when it will be granted.

進度確認

Please help me check my visa application progress and let me know if I need to provide any further documents.

Hope to hear from you soon,
Benson Chu

段落大意

目的	開場直接說明你要詢問簽證的近況。
細節	告知簽證申請時間和細節。
敬請回覆	請對方回覆。
信尾	客套語 + 署名。

中文翻譯

親愛的Wills先生：

我寫這封信是為了詢問我的加拿大旅遊簽證申請進度。我是在12月15日提出申請，申請索引號碼是Z00325。我從你們網路上得知簽證處理時間約需要7到10個工作天。從我申請到現在已經兩個禮拜了，我想知道簽證是否已經核發，或何時會被核發。

請幫我查詢簽證申請現況，讓我知道我是否需要補繳文件。

希望盡速得到您的回覆。

Benson 朱 敬上

換個對象寫寫看

學生簽證延長效期進度

☞ Can you please help me check the status of my student visa application to the U.K.? My visa application reference number is _____. On Dec. 15th I applied to extend my current student visa for another six months, in order to complete my postgraduate programs in London.

您能否幫我檢查我的英國學生簽證申請現況？我的簽證申請索引代號是……。我在12月15日提出簽證延長效期，希望延長6個月效期，以在倫敦完成我的碩士學位。

打工度假簽證進度

☞ I will highly appreciate it if you can check the progress of my Australia working holiday visa? My TRN (transaction reference number) is _____. My application was lodged online on Oct. 2nd, and I have completed health check and submitted the financial statement. Please inform me of the latest status.

若您能協助檢查我的澳洲打工度假簽證申請進度，我將萬分感激。我的交易號碼是……。我在10月2日上網完成線上申請，而且已經完成健康檢查並且繳交財力證明文件。請通知我最新的進度。

其他請求協助確認資訊的句型

☞ I will be very grateful if you can inform me of the progress of my visa application.

若讓您能告知我的簽證申請進度，我將十分感謝。

☞ Can you kindly help confirm if my visa has been issued?

能否請您確認我的簽證是否已經核發下來了？

☞ Would you please notify me of the progress of my visa application? Your efforts will be highly appreciated.

您能否通知我簽證進度？您的協助，我將感激不盡。

句型解說在這裡

句型1

be + p.p. + by + O　被動語態

	主動語態	被動語態
現在簡單式	He waters the flowers every day.	The flowers are watered every day.
過去簡單式	He watered the flowers yesterday.	The flowers were watered yesterday.
現在進行式	He is watering the flowers now.	The flowers are being watered now.
未來簡單式	He will water the flowers tomorrow.	The flowers will be watered tomorrow.
現在完成式	He has watered the flowers already.	The flowers have been watered already.
結合助動詞	He may water the flowers later.	The flowers may be watered later.

句型2

whether S + V (or not) / if + S + V　是否……→間接問句

- Does he live in Taipei?　他是否住在台北。
  → Can you tell me if / whether he lives in Taipei.
  注意：直接問句改成間接問句時，主詞在動詞之前，動詞注意時態變化。
- Does he live in Taipei? → Can you tell me if / whether he lives in Taipei.
- Did he call you last night? → I wonder if / whether he called you last night.
- Have they arrived yet? → I don't know if / whether they have arrived yet.
- Is he ready now? → Let me know if / whether he is ready now.

練習時間試試看

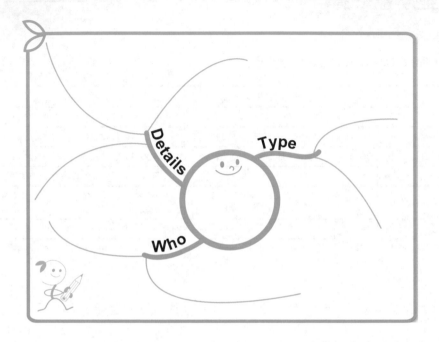

 Step 1 Who are you writing to? 要寫給誰？

 Step 2 What type of visa are you applying for? 你申請哪一種簽證？

 Step 3 Details of visa application 簽證申請書的細節

練習範例分享

To Whom It May Concern,

I'm writing this letter to ask about the status of my

working visa application to China, which was lodged

on Nov. 10th. My application reference number is

CT0352. It's been two weeks since I submitted my

application. I'm wondering if it's still being processed.

Can you kindly inform me when my visa will be

issued.

Thank you for your prompt attention and I look forward

to hearing from you soon.

Sincerely,

Kelly Hsiao

對象

申請書相關

進度確認

敬啟者：

我寫這封信是為了詢問我的大陸工作簽證申請進度。我是在11月10日提出申請，申請索引號碼是CT0352。從我申請到現在已經兩個禮拜了。我想知道簽證申請案是否仍在處理中。可否請您告訴我簽證何時會核發？

感謝您迅速處理我的詢問，期待能盡速收到您的消息。

Kelly 蕭 敬上

情境三 旅客登機資訊確認

心智圖解說

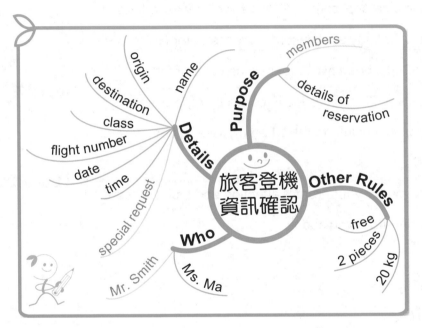

心智圖內容：
- **Details**：origin、destination、class、flight number、date、time、special request、name
- **Purpose**：members、details of reservation
- **Other Rules**：free、2 pieces、20 kg
- **Who**：Mr. Smith、Ms. Ma
- 中心：旅客登機資訊確認

寫作技巧錦囊

Step 1 Who will receive this letter? 誰會收到這封信？
→ Ms. Ma, travel agent

Step 2 What is the purpose of the letter? 這封信的主旨
→ inform details of reservation

Step 3 Details Listed on The Boarding Pass 登機證上的細節
→ name of the passenger; origin; destination; flight number; class; date; time

Step 4 Other Rules 其他規定
→ free; 2 pieces; 20 kg

單字片語搶先看

1. **origin** *n.[C,U]* 起源；由來；起因
   - Please tell the booking agent the origin and destination of your round trip.
   請告知訂票人員你的來回機票出發地點和目的地。
   詞類變化：originate *vi. vt.* 發源；引起

2. **boarding gate** 登機門
   - Passengers to Flight No. T312, please go to Boarding Gate No.12. now.
   搭乘T312班機的旅客，請現在前往12號登機門。

3. **aisle** *n.[C]* 走道
   - Most travelers prefer window seats to aisle seats for the view.
   大部分的旅客，因為視野的關係，偏愛靠窗的座位勝過靠走道的座位。

4. **economic** 經濟艙
   - A free airline upgrade to business class or first class is the holy grail for many travellers.
   對很多旅客來說，從經濟艙免費升等到商務艙或頭等艙是他們渴望得到的優惠。
   延伸字彙：business 商務艙；first class頭等艙

5. **itinerary** *n.[C]* 路線 *(= schedule, timetable)*
   - Please leave me a copy of your itinerary in case of emergency.
   請讓我保留一份你的旅遊行程表，以防萬一。

6. **carry-on luggage** 隨身行李
   - Each passenger is allowed to take one piece of carry-on luggage of less than 10 kg.
   每位乘客可以帶一件10公斤內的隨身行李。

7. **allowance** *n.[C]* 允許
   - Sales staff get a generous mileage allowance.
   業務員得到大額度的里程津貼。

英文範例

【★可替換其他對象或情境】

對象：旅行代辦業者

Dear Ms. Chou,

★ I'm very pleased to inform you we've completed the flight reservation for Ms. Chen Mei-Ru. The following are the details of your reservation. ——— 對象

Name of the Passenger: Ms. Chen Mei-Ru

Origin: Taipei, Taiwan (R.O.C)

Destination: New York, the U.S.A.

Flight Number: B3120

Class: economic

Date and Time of Departure: 08:15, Sep. 9th, 2012 ——— 旅客登機資訊

★ The flight itinerary will be sent to your email address. Please forward to your client and confirm the above information.

Please also inform Ms Chen of the following rules.

1. Please arrive at the airport at least 2 hours prior to the boarding time.

2. Each passenger is permitted one piece of carry-on luggage.

3. Free baggage allowance:

(1) Piece：2pieces

(2) Weight：Each piece must not weigh more than 20 kg. ——— 注意事項

Thank you.

Sincerely,

Jenny Lai

段落大意

破題　　開場直接說明以下提供旅客的登機資料。

旅客登機資料　詳述登機時間、班機資訊。

注意事項　提醒登機須注意事項。

信尾　　客套語 + 署名。

中文翻譯

親愛的Ms. Chou:

我們很開心通知您：您幫陳美如小姐預定的機票已經訂好了。以下是登機資料：

旅客姓名：陳美如	艙　　等：經濟艙
出 發 地：台灣台北	班機號碼：B3120
目 的 地：美國紐約	出發日期與時間：2012年9月9日，上午8點15分

班機行程表會寄發到您的電子信箱。請與客戶確認以上資料正確。
也請轉達陳小姐以下登機規定：
1. 請在登機時間前2個小時抵達機場。
2. 每位旅客只能攜帶一件隨身行李。
3. 免費托運行李：
(1) 兩件
(2) 個別重量在20公斤以下。

感謝您。

Jenny 賴　敬上

換個對象寫寫看

【★可替換其他對象或情境】

更改訂位紀錄

With reference to your previous E-mail requesting changing the departure time / date, we'd like to inform you the reservation has been amended to your needs. Here are the details. Please also be aware that we charge $50 change fee.

關於您上次來信提到要更改班機啟程日期與時間，要通知您我們已經依照您的需求更改訂位紀錄了。

以下是登機細節。請注意我們會收取50美金的訂位更改手續費。

信用卡付費確認訂位

To complete the flight reservation, please offer the following payment information.
Credit card type
Credit card number / expiration date and card verification number
card holder's full name and billing address

為了確認訂位，請提供以下付款資訊：
信用卡卡別
信用卡號碼／失效日期／卡片背面末三碼
持卡人全名與帳單寄送地址

「確認」資料的萬用句型

Can you review the attached <u>boarding details</u> and reply with confirmation?

可否請您過目附件的登機資料細節並回信確認？

We'd be much grateful if you can confirm the following / above flight reservation details within 12 hours upon receiving this mail.

若您能在收到此信12小時內，確認以下／以上的班機訂位資訊，我們將十分感激。

Please kindly check the enclosed flight reservation details and confirm if the information is correct at your earliest convenience.

請查閱附件的班機訂位資訊，並請盡速撥冗確認資料是否正確無誤。

句型解說在這裡

句型1

> the above 以上的
> the following 以下的
> →the above / the following後面的動詞，以後方名詞的單複數決定
> 　動詞單複數。

- The following / above are the tips for this middle-age woman to stay young.
  以下／以上是這位中年美女維持年輕的秘訣。
- The following are the tips to make your ends meet.
  以下是維持收支平衡的一些秘訣。
- The above is the his explanation to the economic downturn.
  以上是他對經濟衰退原因的解釋。

句型2

prior to + N　　在……之前

- Please make the payment at least 3 days prior to the departure time.
  請在啟程日前3天完成付費。

延伸觀念

「在……之前」相關片語
1. in advance / before hand：放在動詞之後或句尾
   - You need to file your leaving request one week in advance.
     你必須在一週前提出請假申請／需求。

2. before：連接兩個句子作為連接詞
   - You need to file the request one week before you take the day off.
     你要在休假一週前提出申請。

練習時間試試看

航空公司訂票員將班機資訊寄給旅客確認

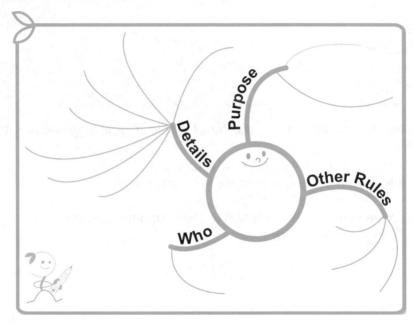

 Who wrote this letter?　對象？

 Who will receive this letter?　收信者？

 Details Listed on The Boarding Pass　登機細節

 Other Details　其他細節

練習範例分享

Dear Ms. Wang,

Thank you very much for booking a flight with Best Airlines. We've completed your flight reservation. The details are as follows. Since you are an honored member of Best Airlines, we're very pleased to inform you that you have been upgraded to fly in business class for your trip to Hong Kong.

> 對象

Name of the Passenger: Ms Cindy Wang

Origin: Taipei, Taiwan (R.O.C)

Destination: Hong Kong, China

Flight Number: B580

Class: business

Date and Time of Departure: 17:15, Dec. 31, 2012

★ The flight itinerary will be sent to your E-mail address. Please confirm the above information.

> 登機細節

Thank you again for flying with us and we look forward to serving you soon.

Regards,

Mandy Chou

> 寫信者

親愛的王小姐：

謝謝您選擇向倍斯特航空訂位，我們已為您訂好機位了，細節如下。由於您是倍斯特航空的貴客，很開心通知您我們已為您免費升等，讓您乘坐商務艙去香港。

旅客姓名：Cindy Wang

出發地：台灣台北

目的地：香港

班機號碼：B580

艙等：商務艙

出發日期與時間：2012年12月31日，下午5點15分

班機行程表會寄發到您的電子信箱。請確認以上資料是否正確。

再次感謝您搭乘倍斯特航空，期待很快再為您服務。

Mandy 周 敬上

Unit 2

訂房

情境一
詢問房間配備、
大小及房價

情境二
預定房間大小事

情境三
加床服務

情境一　詢問房間配備、大小及房價

心智圖解說

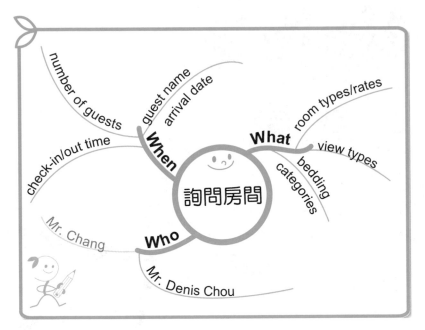

（心智圖文字）

number of guests　guest name　arrival date

check-in/out time

When

room types/rates

What

view types

bedding categories

詢問房間

Mr. Chang

Who

Mr. Denis Chou

寫作技巧錦囊

Who are writing to?　對象？
→ Mr. Denis Chou

When are you going to stay at the hotel?　何時入住？
→ Arrival Date; Departure Date; Number of Guests; Check-in Time;
Check-out Time

What do you want to know about accommodation?
你想知道的房間資訊
→ Room types; bedding categories; view types; amenities; room
rates

單字片語搶先看

1. **intend** *vt.* 計畫；企圖
   - I intend to spend the night at a youth hostel in the suburb.
   我計畫要在郊區的一間青年旅館過夜。
   詞類變化intention *n.[C]*

2. **period** *n.[C]* 期間
   - a period of time一段期間
   - His English has improved in a very short period of time.
   他的英文在短期間之內進步很快。

3. **forward** *vt.* 寄發 *(= send)*
   - I received a joke and forwarded it to all my close friends in no time.
   我收到一則笑話，立刻轉寄給我的好友們。

4. **rate** *n.[C]* 價格；費率 *(= price)*
   - Some hotels offer special rates for children and seniors.
   部分飯店會提供孩童或老人住房優惠。

5. **description** *n.[C]* 解說；描述
   - The police have issued a detailed description of the missing woman.
   警方發布關於這位失蹤女子的詳細描述。

6. **amenities** *n. [plural]* 設備；設施
   - A standard room comes with basic amenities, bedding and furnishing.
   飯店標準房間提供基本的設備、床組以及傢俱。

7. **size** *n.[C]* 尺寸大小
   - The average size of standard guestrooms is around 300 to 400 feet square.
   一間標準客房的平均面積約為300到400平方英尺。

8. **availability** *n.[C]* 可得到性
   - I'm writing to enquire room availability at your hotel in July and August.
   我寫這封信目的是詢問貴旅館七月和八月是否仍有房間。
   詞類變化：available *adj.*

英文範例

【★可替換其他需求】

請旅館經理提供房間配備、大小及房價

Dear Mr. Denis Chou,   ● 對象

★I will be coming to Dubai on a business tour for one

week from May 15th to May 21st, and I intend to book   ● 時間

a room in your hotel for this period. Please kindly

forward your rates for various types of accommodation,

with descriptions of room amenities and sizes. Please

also let me know the availability on the dates I have

mentioned, and whether you can book a room for me   ● 房間資訊

in advance.

Thank you for your attention and I look forward to

hearing from you soon.

Yours sincerely,

Ned Smith

段落大意

住房日期　　開場告知有住房需要，說明入住時間和需求房間數。

提出需求　　請對方提供房間配備、大小及房價表。

敬請回覆　　請對方回信。

信尾　　　　客套語 + 署名。

中文翻譯

Denis Chou先生您好：

我將會來杜拜出差一週，時間是在5月15日到21日，這段期間我計畫在你們的飯店訂一間房。煩請您寄給我不同房型的房價，並請附上房間設備和大小的說明。也請讓我知道我上述提到的時間是否有房位，以及您能否幫我預先預定房間。

謝謝您處理以上事宜，希望能盡速收到您的回覆。

Ned Smith　敬上

換個對象寫寫看

祕書幫主管訂位

This is to enquire about the availability of accommodation in your hotel in November. Our Managing Director and his wife are scheduled to visit Dubai for 7 days and intend to stay at your hotel from November 15 to 21th. Please confirm reservation of a double deluxe room.

我寫這封信是想詢問貴飯店11月住房是否還有房位。我們的常務董事與夫人預定要拜訪杜拜7天，希望在你們飯店下榻，期間是11月15到21日。請確認預訂一間豪華雙人房。

透過旅行社業者代為訂房

I've learned from your website that I can book a room at the Ritz in Dubai with discounted rates via your agency. I'm traveling to Dubai on a short transfer for about two months in the beginning of April and I would like you to help book a single standard room at the Ritz.

我從你們網站上得知貴旅行社可以代為向杜拜麗池酒店訂房，並提供優惠住房價格。我四月初將會調職到杜拜2個月，這段期間我計畫透過你們代為向杜拜麗池酒店訂一間單人標準房。

其他詢問房間配備、飯店設施的萬用語

Please provide me with your tariff, details of room sizes and amenities offered.
請提供我你們的房間價目表，房間大小和房間設備等細節。

We would like to enquire about your hotel's packages, charges, as well as the services and facilities that are provided.
我們想詢問你們有關貴飯店的服務配套、費用，以及你們提供的服務和設施。

Please kindly let us have illustrated leaflets or brochures, price lists and the facilities. I'd also like to know if there are any special rates or packages.
請提供你們的宣傳單或手冊，以及住房價格和飯店設施介紹。我也想知道是否有住房優惠或優惠方案。

It's highly appreciated if we can obtain more information about prices and discounts for accommodation, facilities and services.
若能取得更多住房價目、優惠方案、飯店設施與服務的資訊，我們將十分感謝。

句型解說在這裡

句型1

`to + VR`

不定詞「to + VR」常做為以下動詞之受詞：afford, agree, aim, arrange, ask / demand / get, choose / decide, deserve, seem, know / learn (how), need / want / would like, intend / plan

- The celebrity intends to file a law suit against the tabloid and paparazzi.
  這位名人打算對八卦小報和狗仔隊提出控告。

延伸句型：

S +	allow / permit ask / get / tell cause choose	convince / persuade instruct / teach remind invite	+ O + to V

- He asked the tabloid to stop prying his privacy.
  他要求八卦媒體不要再窺探他的隱私。

句型2

`to + V-ing`

觀念：以下片語中的to是介系詞，後面的動詞要用V-ing形式：
- look forward to（期待）、adapt to（適應）、be opposed to（反對）、be used to（習慣）、be devoted / dedicated to（致力於）、when it comes to（說到／提到）
- I'm used to eating alone at home. But I look forward to eating out with my friends this weekend.
  我習慣一個人在家吃飯。但我期待這週末和我朋友出去吃飯。

練習時間試試看

請旅館經理提供房間配備、大小及房價

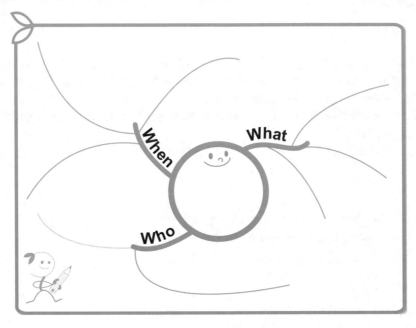

 Who are you writing to?　對象？

 When are you going to stay at the hotel?　何時？

 What do you want to know about accommodation?
關於住宿想知道？

練習範例分享

To the Manager,　　　　　　　　　　　　　　　　　　　● 對象

I'm writing to inquire more information for my stay at

your hotel from July 18th to 20th. I'd like to know the

rates for a single standard room, and get further details　● 何時

about room amenities and sizes. Please also let me

know if there are rooms available on the dates I have

mentioned.　　　　　　　　　　　　　　　　　　　● 關於住宿想知道

Thank you and I look forward to your prompt reply.

Yours faithfully,

Peter Kao

經理您好：

我寫這封信目的是要詢問更多關於我下榻貴飯店的資訊，下榻日期為7月18日到20日。我想要知道標準單人房的房價，以及更多關於房間設備和大小的細節。也請讓我知道我上述提到的時間是否有房位。

謝謝您，希望能盡速收到您的回覆。

Peter 郭　敬上

情境二　預定房間大小事

心智圖解說

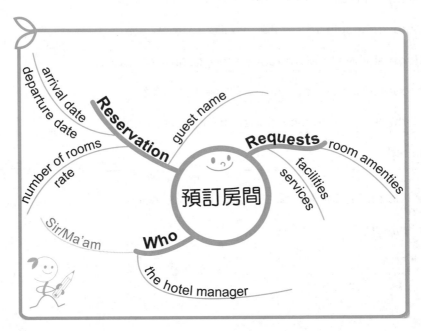

寫作技巧錦囊

Who are you writing to?　對象？
→ the hotel manager

The information of making a room **reservation**　訂房資訊
→ Guest Name; Arrival Date; Departure Date; Number of rooms; Accommodations; Rate per Night

detailed **requests / requirements** of your stay　詳細的住房需求
→ Room amenities; Facilities & services;

單字片語搶先看

1. **incentive tour** 員工旅遊 incentive *adj.* 激勵的
   - The employees get to vote for the destination and package for their annual incentive tour.
   這些員工可以投票決定年度員工旅遊的目的地以及行程。

2. **duration** *n.[U]* 期間
   - The course of Hotel Management is of three-month duration.
   這一門旅館管理的課程為期三個月。
   詞類變化：during *prep.* 在……期間

3. **current** *adj.* 現在的 *(= present)*
   - In its current state, the car is worth NT$100,000.
   以這部車現在的車況來看，它價值十萬元。

4. **well-furnished** *adj.* 裝潢很好的
   - We enjoyed a pleasant weekend at the well-furnished family room.
   我們在這裝潢良好的家族套房度過很棒的週末。

5. **separate** *adj.* 分開的，分別的 *(=divided)*
   - The kids stay in separate rooms, each with a computer.
   孩子們待在不同的房間，每間都有自己的電腦。

6. **wireless** *adj.* 無線的
   - The city government provides free wireless access to the Internet in public areas.
   市政府在公共地區提供無線上網服務。

7. **level** *n.[C]* 層樓，級數 *(=floor, ground)*
   - Didn't we park the car on Level 2?
   我們難道不是把車停在第二層嗎？

英文範例

【★可替換不同訂房需求】

團體訂房，提出住房需求

Dear Sir / Ma'am,

Our company has decided to stay at your hotel for our incentive tour on December 20th, 2012, for a duration of 3 days. We plan to book 30 rooms to accommodate an approximate number of 80 people. Prior to our confirmation, we would like to know about tourist group packages. Please send me the list room types and current group rates.

★ Our requests for accommodation are as follows. We prefer well-furnished suites, with separate bath and toilet, and wireless Internet in each room. We also want rooms on lower level floor. And can you get us rooms next to each other?

I would appreciate it if you can reply to the above inquiries by tomorrow.

Regards,

Frank Chian

the HR manager of IBM Corporation

— 對象

— 訂房資訊

— 詳細的住房需求

段落大意

訂房需求	開場直接說明你要訂房，簡述房間數量，下榻日期。
需求細節	告知對方所需提供的服務。
敬請回覆	請對方回覆。
信尾	客套語 + 署名。

中文翻譯

親愛的先生／女士：

我們公司已決定今年員工旅遊要在貴酒店住房，從2012年12月20日起下榻3天。我們計畫訂30間房，以容納大約80人。在我們確認下訂前，我們想知道團體旅客住房方案。請給我們房型列表和現在的團體住房房價。

以下是我們的住房要求。我們希望訂裝潢舒適的套房，淋浴間和廁所隔開，每間房都要能無線上網。我們也想要低樓層的房間，此外可否請您讓我們的房間集中彼此相鄰？

若您能在明天前回覆以上詢問，我將十分感激。

IBM公司人資經理
Frank 簡 敬上

換個對象寫寫看

房間內部設備

⊙ I'd like to book a deluxe suite with ocean view. I hope it can also be equipped with high-speed Internet access, flat screen color television and home theater. Please also provide an iron and ironing board. I also want a Jacuzzi in the bathing area.

我想要預訂有海景的豪華套房，我希望房間可以高速上網，配備有平板彩色電視和家庭劇院組。也請提供熨斗和燙衣板。我也想要浴室裡有按摩浴缸。

飯店設施與服務

⊙ Since I'm traveling with my wife and two children under the age of five, I'd like to request for babysitting and child-care services during the day while we're out for sightseeing. I'd like to make an appointment with your spa salon for my wife so she can enjoy the manicure, pedicure, facial and whole-body massage services.

因為我和我太太以及兩個5歲以下的孩童一起出遊，我們想要白天出外觀光時，請你們協助看護孩童。我也要幫我太太向你們的水療沙龍預約，這樣她就可以享用你們的美甲、作臉以及全身按摩等服務。

其他訂房要求的萬用句型

⊙ A small but decently furnished and well-ventilated room would be quite enough for me.
一個小但裝潢精美且通風良好的房間對我來說就足夠了。
⊙ I would prefer an accommodation on the ground floor.
我偏好一樓的房間。
⊙ Please confirm reservation for one double bed / single bed room with air-conditioning.
請確認幫我預訂一個雙人床／單人床房間，附有空調冷氣。
⊙ I will need a bath attached single room.
我需要一間附衛浴的單人房。

句型解說在這裡

句型1

a number of + 可數名詞複數形
an amount of + 不可數名詞

數量為……

- The science team is working on a large number of experiments.
  這個科學團隊正在進行為數眾多的實驗。
- USB technology benefits a huge number of gadgets.
  隨插即用的科技造福大量的電子產品。
- A large amount of money was stolen from the bank.
  大量的金錢從這家銀行被竊取。

句型2

......is / are as follows

……如下

- The winners are as follows: Mandy, Sandy, and Hannah.
  = The following are the winners, Mandy, Sandy, and Hannah.
  優勝者如下：Mandy, Sandy還有Hannah。
  →注意：as follows / the following 搭配的 be動詞依據提及的名詞單複數作變化。
- The reasons why I am against smoking are as follows.
  我反對抽菸的理由如下。
- The result of the competition is as follows.
  比賽結果如下。

練習時間試試看

為外國友人訂房，提出住房需求

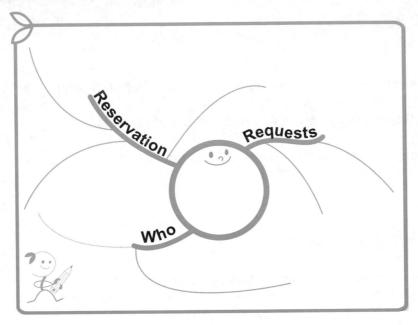

 Who are you writing to?　對象？

 Make a room **reservation**　訂房資訊

 detailed **requests** / **requirements** of your stay
詳細的住房需求

練習範例分享

Dear Sir / Ma'am,

對象

I'm arranging a trip for my two Japanese clients, Mr. Ichiro
Takashi and Mr. Davishi Kenji, I'd like to book a deluxe
twin room for them to stay at your hotel from Feb 5 to 7.

訂房資訊

Their requests for accommodation are as follows. They
hope the room can be equipped with a / c, broadband
Internet access, coffee and tea making facilities, and
an LCD TV with Satellite Channels. They also request
for taxis to shopping and sightseeing destinations.
They also like to have an interpreter for their day tour
on Feb 6th.

詳細的訂房

Can you reply to me if you can meet the above
requests as soon as possible?

Hope to hearing from you soon,
Belle Hsieh

親愛的先生／女士：

我正在幫我的兩個日本客戶Ichiro Takashi 和Davishi Kenji先生安排旅遊行程。我想
要訂一間兩床的房間，讓他們在2月5日到7日期間在你們旅館下楊。以下是他們的住
房要求。他們希望房間有空調、寬頻上網、咖啡或茶水沖泡設備，以及可收看衛星
頻道的液晶電視。他們也要求你們可以提供接駁車載他們去購物或觀光景點，也希
望2月6日的旅遊能有口譯人員陪同。

您能盡速回覆是否能滿足以上需求嗎？

期待盡快得到您的回覆

Belle 謝 敬上

情境三　加床服務

心智圖解說

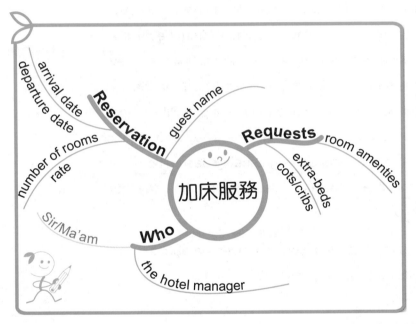

寫作技巧錦囊

Who are you writing to?　對象
→ the hotel manager

Make a room **reservation**　預訂房間
→ Guest Name; Arrival Date; Departure Date; Number of rooms; Accommodations; Rate per Night

Request for extra-beds / cots / cribs and / or children　需求

單字片語搶先看

1. **check in** *phr.* 住房登記
   - Most hotels allow customers to check in after 3:00 pm.
   大部分飯店讓顧客下午三點以後辦住房登記。

2. **check out** *phr.* 退房手續
   - Customers need to complete check-out procedures by 12:00 pm..
   顧客要在中午12點前辦妥退房手續。

3. **policy** *n.[C]* 法規 *(= regulation, rule)*
   - Cancellation and prepayment policies vary according to room type.
   訂房取消或預繳訂金的規定依訂房房型不同而有所差別。

4. **accept** *vi. vt.* 接受
   - Only a few hotels can accept last-minute cancellation of reservation.
   只有少數旅館可以接受最後一刻取消訂房。

5. **extra** *adj.* 額外的
   - Any type of extra bed or cot is upon request and needs to be confirmed by the hotel.
   任何形式的追加床組或搖床都必須先提出申請，且要經過飯店同意。

6. **charge** *vi.vt.* 收費；索價 (也可當名詞)
   - One child over 12 years old or adult is charged NT$ 800 per night and person in an extra bed.
   12歲以上兒童或成人，每加一床每晚要多付800元。

7. **add** *vi.vt.* 增加
   - Maximum capacity of extra beds / children's cots in a room is 1.
   每間房最多追加一張床或兒童搖床。

英文範例

【★可替換不同加床需求或確認兒童同行收費規定】

夫妻訂房，提出為7歲兒童加床需求

Dear Sir / Ma'am,　　　　　　　　　　　　　　　　　● 對象

My wife and I plan to book our stay at your hotel for our

family trip to Hualian. We'd like to check in on June 21st

and check out on the 23rd (2 nights). Please reserve a

standard double room for our stay-over. ★ Considering　● 預訂房間

our 7-year-old daughter will be staying with us, too,

we would like to know about your policies for children

sharing the room with parents. Do you accept our

request for an extra bed? If it's OK, how much do you

charge for adds-on beds?　　　　　　　　　　　　　● 需求

Your early reply to the above matters will be highly

appreciated.

Warm regards,

Peter Jennings

段落大意

訂房需求	開場直接說明你要訂房，簡述房間數量，下榻日期。
提出加床需求	詢問對方可否加床以及是否額外收費。
敬請回覆	請對方回覆。
信尾	客套語 ＋ 署名。

中文翻譯

親愛的先生／女士：

我太太和我打算到花蓮旅行時，在貴旅館過2晚。我們打算6月21日下榻，23日離開。請幫我們訂一間標準雙人房。考慮到我們7歲的女兒會同行，我們想知道你們針對兒童和父母同住一間的收費規定。你們可否接受我們要求加一張床？如果可以的話，收多少額外的費用？

若您能盡速回覆以上事項，我們將不勝感激。

Peter Jennings 敬上

換個對象寫寫看

幫嬰幼兒加嬰兒床或兒童搖床

◌ Since we are taking our 2-year-old baby girl with us, I'd like to request for an extra crib / cot in our room.
因為我們會帶我們的兩歲女兒同行，我想要求在房間內多準備一張嬰兒床或兒童搖床。

◌ Please let me know if the extra cot / crib is available. I look forward to your confirmation.
請讓我知道你們可否提供嬰兒床或兒童搖床，我等候你們的回覆確認。

確認加床不加價的服務是否屬實

◌ I've checked your hotel policies from your website. It says children are allowed to stay in the room with parents either with or without an extra bed with NO EXTRA charge if they are under twelve years of age. I'd like to confirm if my acknowledgement to the above policies is correct. If yes, please book one extra bed for our 10-year-old son.
我看過你們網站的住房規定。規定上寫說兒童可以和父母同住一間房（可加床或不加床），且12歲以下的兒童免加收費用。我想確認我對該規定的理解是否正確。如果無誤，我想幫同行的10歲兒子加一張床。

其他加床要求的相關問句

◌ Can you inform me of your hotel policies regarding children sharing rooms and extra bed requests?
可否請您告知有關兒童同住一間房或加床的收費規定。

◌ Will you charge for an extra bed for children under 7 years old?
你們會針對7歲以下幼兒加床多收費用嗎？

◌ Your hotel policies say that children above the age of 12 or adults will pay NT$800 per person, per night in an extra bed. Please confirm.
你們住房規定上寫說12歲以上兒童或成人，每加一床每晚要多付800元。請確認。

◌ Your concierge told me breakfast is not included for children when sharing a room with their parents. In such cases, I'd like to know how you will charge for the child's breakfast?
你們櫃檯人員告訴我與父母同行的兒童無法享用免費的早餐服務。在這種情況下，我想知道孩童的早餐如何收費？

句型解說在這裡

句型1

介係詞「for + 名詞」常見涵義

1. 為了……;因為　　　表「目的、原因」
- Please reserve a standard double room for our stay-over.
  請幫我們訂一間標準雙人房。
2. 對於……關於　　　　表「主題,對象」
- I'd like to know about your hotel policies for children.
  我想要了解關於兒童住房的規定。
3. 達, 計　　　　　　　表「時間、距離」
- He has been watching TV for an hour.
  他已經看了一個小時的電視。
4. 當作　　　　　　　　表「代表、作為」
- We use boxes for chairs.
  我們用紙箱當椅子。
5. 贊成　　　　　　　　表「支持」
- More than 30% of the citizens are for death penalty.
  超過三成的公民贊同死刑。
6. 朝向　　　　　　　　表「方向」
- He left / headed for Taipei last night.
  他昨晚前往台北。

句型2

介係詞「to + 名詞」常見涵義

1. 往、到、向　　　　　　表「方向」
- He went to Taipei with his friends for a trip.
  他和朋友去台北旅遊。
2. (變)成,(變)到　　表「轉變、趨勢」
- Things went from bad to worse.
  情勢愈來愈糟。
3. 直到、達　　　　　表「時間、程度、範圍」
- He worked from day to midnight.
  他從早工作到午夜。
4. 對、向　　　　　　表「對象」
- He handed in his resignation letter to his supervisor.
  他遞交辭呈給長官。
5. 屬於　　　　　　　表「歸屬」
- I bought a ticket to the concert, but lost my key to the door.
  我買了演唱會門票,卻把家門鑰匙搞丟。

練習時間試試看

三個友人同行，只訂一間雙人房（兩張單人床），要求加一床

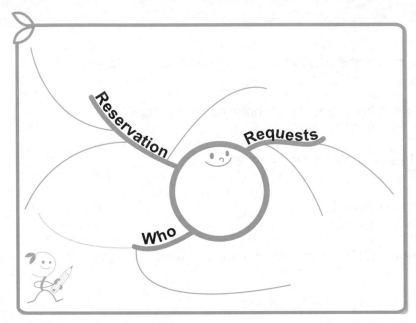

 Who are you writing to?　對象？

 Make a room **reservation**　預訂房間

 Request for extra-beds / cots / cribs and / or children　需求

練習範例分享

To the hotel manager,

→ 對象

Two of my friends and I are planning to stay at your hotel for one night on Saturday, May 5th. Please kindly book a deluxe twins room for our stay-over. Since

→ 預訂房間

there are three of us sharing one room, we would like to know about your policies for extra beds. Is it OK to book one extra bed in our twins room? If that's fine, can you tell us how you will charge the extra bed?

→ 需求

Thank you and we look forward to your earliest reply.

Sincerely,

Sandy Summers

飯店經理您好：

我和我兩個朋友計畫要在5月5日週六在你們旅館下榻一晚。煩請幫我們訂一間豪華雙人房（兩張單人床）。因為我們三個人要同住一間房，想要知道你們對於加床的收費規定。我們可以在雙人房裡加一張床嗎？如果可以的話，能否請您告知如何收費？

感謝您，也期待您能盡快回覆。

Sandy Summers 敬上

Unit 3

投訴

情境一
抱怨服務人員
態度不佳

情境二
廚師做菜很難吃

情境三
抱怨新買的智慧型
手機又出問題了

情境一　抱怨服務人員態度不佳

心智圖解說

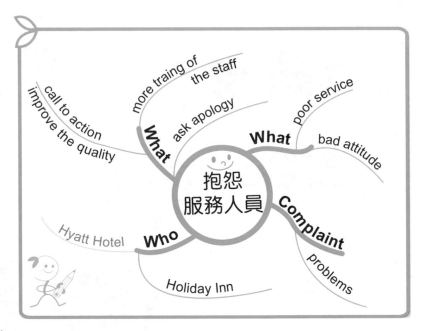

寫作技巧錦囊

Who are you writing to?　對象？
→ Holiday Inn

What do you complain about?　抱怨什麼？
→ poor service / incompetence and bad attitude of the personnel towards the customer

Details of the complaint　抱怨細節
→ problems

What would you like the recipient to do?　你想要接待人員做什麼？
→ call to action improve the quality of service / more training of the staff / ask for proper apology from the personnel / company

單字片語搶先看

1. **loyal** *adj.* 忠實的
   - Loyal customers keep coming back to the restaurant for its outstanding services and good quality food.

   該餐廳因為有優越的服務品質和高水準的食物，讓忠實顧客不斷回籠。

   詞類變化：loyalty *n.[U]* 忠誠度

2. **emphasis** *n.[C,U]* 強調；重視；重點
   - His English teacher puts emphasis on his reading proficiency.

   他的英文老師很注重他的閱讀能力。

   詞類變化：emphasize *vt.* 強調 (+ on ...)

3. **recent** *adj.* 最近的 (= the latest)
   - This recent news has triggered some heated debate.

   這則最近的新聞引發了熱烈的辯論。

4. **plumbing** *n.[U]* 配管工程
   - We keep having problems with the plumbing.

   我們的水管一直出問題。

   詞類變化：plumb *n.[C]* 水管　plumber *n.[C]* 修水管工人

5. **faulty** *adj.* （產品）有問題的
   - Customers may ask for a refund if the goods are faulty.

   若產品有問題，顧客可能要求退費。

6. **complain** *vi.vt.* 抱怨 (+about某事；+ to 某人)
   - The tenant complained to the landlord about the malfunction of the air-conditioner.

   這位房客向房東抱怨冷氣故障。

   詞類變化：complaint *n.[C,U]* 抱怨；抗議；怨言

7. **to make things worse** 更糟的是
   - The team has lost a series of games. To make things worse, its best pitcher got hurt yesterday.

   這球隊連輸了幾場比賽。更糟的是，隊上最好的投手昨天受傷了。

英文範例

【★可替換其他抱怨細節】

請旅館經理提供房間配備、大小及房價

To the Hotel Manager,

I am a frequent traveler and have been a loyal customer of your hotel for many years because I appreciate your emphasis on excellent service. But a recent episode at your hotel has made me question my loyalty.

對象

★ I stayed in your hotel, room 203, from Monday, September 1th through Thursday, September 4. Throughout my stay my towels were always dirty, and the bathroom plumbing was faulty. To make matters worse, one of my neighbors was very loud at night. I complained to the Front Desk Manager, Annie Shao, and requested another room but was told there were no other rooms available. Despite my repeated complaints, it was not until the third day of my stay that the plumbing was fixed and my towels changed. And no one from the hotel spoke to my noisy neighbor. Because of the noise, I was unable to sleep comfortably for two nights.

抱怨的細節

I hope this problem will be corrected prior to my next visit. Thanks for your time and patience.

想要接待人員
做什麼

Sincerely,

Jenny Chen

段落大意

寫信目的	開場可直接點名是來抱怨，或先說自己原本有很高期待，但卻得到令人失望的產品或服務。
問題核心	以陳述事實的口吻，點出服務不周之處或產品的瑕疵。
敬請回覆	要求對方退換貨 / 退款，或純粹要求對方下次要改進。
信尾	客套語 + 署名。

中文翻譯

飯店經理您好：

我是個飛行常客，多年來是貴旅館的忠實顧客，因為我很欣賞你們強調高品質的服務，但最近一起事件讓我開始質疑我對你們的忠誠度。

我在9月1日（週一）到9月4日（週四）在貴旅館下榻四天，這段期間內，我的毛巾永遠都是髒的，廁所馬桶也不通。更糟的是，隔壁的房客晚上總是很吵。我有和櫃檯經理Annie Shao抱怨過，並要求換房，但我被告知沒有房間可換，且儘管我不斷反應，一直拖到下榻後三天，我的房間廁所才被修好，毛巾才換新。且飯店都沒有人幫我和隔壁的房客作溝通。因為噪音的關係，我有兩天晚上無法好好入睡。

我希望這個問題在我下次造訪前能有所改善。
謝謝您的時間和耐心。

Jenny 陳　敬上

換個對象寫寫看

服務人員態度不佳

- I would like to air my complaints about the very poor service that I received at your hotel, from the 1st of September to the 4th. I was unhappy with the staff's attitude. When I called the concierge and asked for room service, he forgot my request and thus failed to deliver my food. When I complained to him, he seemed indifferent and wasn't willing to fix the error.

  我想要寫信抱怨9月1日到4日我在貴旅館下榻期間,你們服務品質低落,服務人員的態度讓我很不高興。當我打電話向櫃檯提出點餐需求時,他忘了我的點餐,因此沒有將餐點送到我房間。當我跟他抱怨時,他態度愛理不理,沒有誠意要處理問題。

服務人員訓練或專業度不足

- I'm writing to complain that your hotel staff portrayed a large amount of incompetence and lack of professionalism during my stay from the 1st of September to the 4th. After the bellman took my baggage to my room, I found the edges of one baggage slightly damaged for being dragged along on the floor. Besides, the cleaning staff often forgot to change my towels and they even forgot to lock the door when they left.

  我寫信來抱怨在我9月1日到4日下榻貴旅館期間,你們旅館人員不斷呈現他們的無能和缺乏專業。當門房幫我把行李搬到房間時,我發現其中一個行李箱邊緣有輕微損傷,應該是因為在地板上拖行造成的。此外,清潔人員常忘了替換毛巾,甚至離開房間時忘了鎖門。

其他抱怨信常見的萬用語

1. My major / main complaint is about the poor service I received during my stay at your hotel.
   我主要的抱怨是在貴旅館下榻時,我得到的服務品質極差。
2. I'm not content with / satisfied with / happy with / very frustrated about / disappointed about the poor services provided during my stay.
   我很不高興／不滿意／不開心／很灰心／很失望在我下榻期間,你們所提供的服務品質很差。

句型解說在這裡

句型1

despite + N 儘管

☞ Despite all our efforts to save the school, the authorities decided to close it.
儘管我們盡全力想要挽救這所學校，政府當局還是決定要關閉它。

延伸觀念

despite = in spite of = regardless of：後面接「名詞」

☞ He went to school despite / in spite of / regardless of the heavy rain.
儘管／雖然下大雨，他還是去上學。

although = despite the fact that：後面接「子句」

☞ He went to school although / despite of the fact it rained heavily.
儘管／雖然下大雨，他還是去上學。

句型2

it is / was not until…… that…… 直到……才……

☞ It is not until one gets sick that he understands the importance of health.
= One doesn't understand the importance of health until he gets sick.
直到生病了，人才會了解健康的重要性。

延伸觀念

強調句句型「It is / was......that......」，將原本句子裡要強調的部分放在is / was後面

The customer complained about the leak to the hotel manager at midnight.	
(強調主詞the customer)	It was the customer that complained about the leak...
(強調受詞about the leak)	It was about the leak that the customer complained to the manager...
(強調受詞to the manager)	It was to the manager that the customer complained about the leak...
(強調時間副詞at night)	It was at midnight that the customer complained to the manager...

練習時間試試看

抱怨餐廳服務不周到

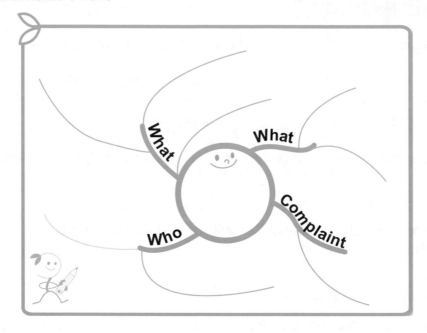

 Who are you writing to?　對象？

 What do you complain about?　抱怨什麼？

 Details of the **complaint**　抱怨細節

 What would you like the recipient to do?
你想要接待人員做什麼？

練習範例分享

To the Heart Restaurant, ● ——————————————● 對象

Up until recently we have enjoyed coming to the Heart
for the food and the service. Unfortunately, after our
visit this past Friday, this view has changed for us.
This past Friday we took our family and friends to the
restaurant. Instead of the usual delightful service, we
encountered problems almost at every turn. The issue
started when our reservation for eight was pushed
back because of overfilled capacity and we were forced
to wait for more than 30 minutes. We were finally given
a round table which was crowded for a group of eight.
The next problem occurred when half of the order was
mixed up and had to be returned.

● ——————————————● 抱怨的細節

Our experience was not near what we had come to
expect from the Heart. Hopefully you will be able to
return to your previous level of excellence.

● ——————————————● 想要接待人員做什麼

Sincerely,
Harvey Harman

甜心餐廳您好：
一直到最近為止，我們都很喜歡到貴餐廳用餐享受美食和服務。但不幸的，我們上
週五用餐的經驗讓我們對於你們的想法有了改觀。

上週五我們帶家人和朋友到貴餐廳，不同於以往的優質服務，我們幾乎每一個環節
都遇到問題。首先是因為客滿的關係，我們八人的訂位被延後了，我們被迫多等30
分鐘。等我們終於有一張桌子後，發現桌子對八個人來說實在太擠。接下來的問題
是我們點的餐點將近一半被弄錯了，必須退回。

我們此行的經驗和我們原本預期得到的不成正比。希望你們能回復之前高品質的服
務水準。

Harvey Harmna 敬上

情境二　廚師做菜很難吃

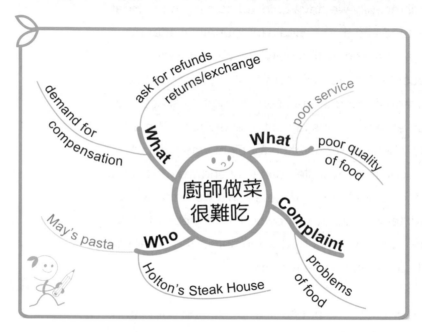

寫作技巧錦囊

Step 1
Who are you writing to?　對象？
→ Holton's Steak House

Step 2
What do you complain about?　抱怨什麼？
→ poor quality of food / dining

Step 3
Details of the complaint　抱怨的細節
→ problems of the food

Step 4
What would you like the recipient to do?　你想要接待人員做什麼？
→ demand for compensation: ask for refunds / returns / exchange / repair of the purchased item / product

單字片語搶先看

1. special *n.[C]* 特餐
   ☞ Thursday's special is rib eye steak.
   週四的特餐是牛肋排。

2. side dish 副餐
   ☞ Today's side dishes include roasted vegetables with smashed potato.
   今天的副餐是烤蔬菜佐馬鈴薯泥。
   相關詞彙：主菜main course, entree

3. serve *vi.vt.* 端菜；供應飯菜
   ☞ The waiter refilled our water before he serves the meal.
   服務生在上菜前幫我們加了點水。
   詞類變化：service *n.[C]* 服務   serving *n.* （食物、飲料）一份

4. rare *adj.* 三分熟的，較生的
   ☞ How do you like your steak? Medium rare, please.
   你的牛排想吃幾分熟？ 5分熟，謝謝。
   相關詞彙：全熟的well-done , 7分熟medium

5. tasteless *adj.* 沒味道的
   ☞ Some children prefer drinks to water because water is tasteless.
   有些小孩比較喜歡喝飲料而不是白開水，因為白開水沒有味道。
   詞類變化：taste *vi.* 品嚐；嚐起來   tasty *adj.* 美味的

6. greasy *adj.* 油膩的
   ☞ To stay fit, this ballerina says no to any greasy food such as fried chicken or hamburgers.
   為維持曼妙身材，這名芭雷舞者拒吃任何油膩食物，例如炸雞和漢堡。

7. diarrhea 腹瀉
   ☞ Many guests had diarrhea after they dined at the wedding banquet in the seafood restaurant.
   很多賓客吃完這間海鮮餐廳辦的喜宴以後，就腹瀉拉肚子。

8. compensate *vi.vt.* 賠償；補償
   ☞ The company compensates the employees for their injuries at work or on duty.
   這間公司對員工在工作或值班期間受傷給予賠償。
   詞類變化：compensation *n.[U]*

英文範例

【★可替換其他抱怨細節】

反應餐點不美味

Dear Sir,

I am writing to air my complaints about the very poor
service that my wife and I received at your restaurant,
on the 1th of August. We were extremely disappointed
with the poor quality of food.

對象

★ On that day I ordered the special, a set containing
soup, steak, side dishes and drinks. And my wife
ordered Seafood Paella. When the meals were served,
we found the food itself was of very poor quality. The
steak's temperature was wrong. It was cold and too rare.
The soup was tasteless. As for the side dishes, the chips
were too greasy and salty, and the vegetables were
cold. My wife complained that her shrimps and scallops
weren't fresh. When we reached home, she suffered
from very bad diarrhea which lasted for two days.
All these things considered, We feel we need to be
compensated. In addition, we demand that the service
be improved at Horton's Steak House. Please contact
me at the following email address:
johnnychen@chenandchang.com to settle this matter.

抱怨什麼

抱怨的細節

賠償的要求

Looking forward to hearing from you soon,

Johnny Chen

段落大意

寫信目的	開場可直接點名是來抱怨,或先說自己原本有很高期待,但卻得到令人失望的產品或服務。
問題核心	以陳述事實的口吻,點出餐點不美味之處。
敬請回覆	要求對方退款或賠償,或純粹要求對方下次要改進。
信尾	客套語 + 署名。

中文翻譯

先生您好:

我要抱怨8月1日我和我太太在貴餐廳用餐時所得到的差勁服務。我們對於餐點品質十分失望。

那天晚上我點了超值餐,包含濃湯、牛排、副餐和飲料的套餐。而我太太點的是西班牙海鮮飯。當餐點送上來,我們發現餐點品質很差。牛排的溫度不對。太冷了而且不夠熟。湯沒有味道。至於副餐部分,薯條太油太鹹,蔬菜也都冷掉了。我老婆則是抱怨她的蝦和干貝都不新鮮。當我們回家後,她拉肚子拉了兩天。

考慮以上所有的問題,我們覺得應該索賠。此外,我們要求貴餐廳改善你們的品質。
請以電子郵件和我聯絡處理這件事,我的電郵信箱:
johnnychen@chenandchang.com。

希望盡速得到您的回覆,

Johnny 陳 敬上

換個對象寫寫看

衛生條件不佳

- During my recent visit to the Hearts I ordered steamed lemon trout. Only moments after starting to eat I noticed a small cockroach in the dish. I immediately felt sick and called over the staff. They apologized and removed my dish and asked me if I wanted something else! I declined to order something else, as my appetite was completely gone. With such an incident, I think the entire meal be made complimentary! I also suggest you examine the cleanliness of the kitchen as well as the food serving areas.

  我最近在貴餐廳用餐時點了清蒸檸檬魚。剛開始用餐就發現裡面有隻小蟑螂。我立刻覺得反胃，並請服務員來查看。他們向我道歉，收回餐點，也問我要不要改點別的，但我因為胃口盡失而拒絕了。因為這起事件，我認為整頓飯應該不計免費。我也建議你們要檢查廚房以及出餐區域的整潔。

餐點送錯或太慢上菜

- The service was very slow. It took nearly an hour for my food to be fully prepared. What made matters worse was that after waiting for so long, our order was mixed up and the waiter brought the wrong food and he had to take it back.

  服務太慢。我點的菜足足花了半個小時才準備好。更糟的是等了老半天後，發現上錯菜了。服務生只好收回再重新出菜。

其他抱怨信常見的萬用語

- I am writing to complain about the unacceptable food quality that I received in your restaurant last Friday when I was intended to have dinner with my husband.

  我寫信來抱怨上週五我和我先生到貴餐廳用餐時，餐點的品質令人無法接受。

- demand compensation because our meal was unsatisfactory.

  因為餐點品質令我很不滿意，我要求賠償。

- I feel I'm entitled to receive compensation due to the poor food quality and lack of hygiene. I demand the entire meal be made complimentary / I wish to deduct the cost of the uneaten dishes. 。

  因為餐點品質和衛生很差，我覺得我有權要求賠償。我要求整頓餐點不計費／沒用到的餐點費用從帳單扣除。

句型解說在這裡

句型1

that + 子句：名詞子句，此子句是前面動詞的受詞

- She complained that the meal was of poor quality. 她抱怨說這頓飯餐點品質不好。
  (that the meal was of poor quality 是前面動詞complain的受詞)

關係代名詞that：在關係子句中，代替前面提到的名詞，可取代who / which

- I was not happy about the poor service. I received the service.
  => I was unhappy with the poor service that (= which) I received.
  我不滿意我受到極差的服務。
  (that 指的就是前面名詞the poor service)

句型2

demand (that) + S + (should) + VR　　要求……應該要……

- The customer demands (that) his meal (should) be compensated.
  顧客要求餐費需被全額賠償。
  (that 子句的that可以省略；所接的子句中的should也可以省略)

延伸其他類似句型

that名詞子句 + S + (should) + VR

| A + | 要求：ask / demand / request
堅持：insist
建議：propose / recommend / suggest / advise
敦促：urge | + that + S + (should) + VR |
| It is | 必要的：necessary / important / vital / essential / imperative
義務的／強制的：mandatory
比較好的：better
急迫的： urgent | + that + S +(should) +VR |

練習時間試試看

抱怨餐廳服務不周到、且餐點品質差

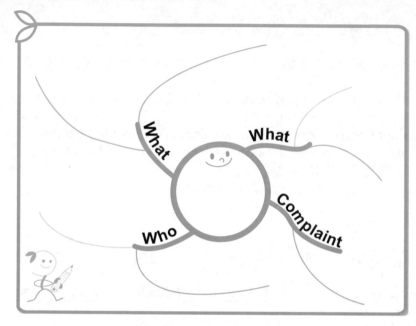

 Who are you writing to?

 What do you complain about?

 Details of the complaint

 What would you like the recipient to do?

練習範例分享

Dear Sir or Madam,
I am writing to complain about the unacceptable treatment that I received in your restaurant last Friday when I had dinner with my husband. — 對象

First of all, we were given a table just in front of the toilets because there was not any other available, although we had booked it in advanced. Secondly, we had to wait for nearly half an hour to be served. To make matters worse, the steak we ordered was over cooked and the salad was warm. Furthermore, we were forced to leave at 9 p.m. because someone else had also booked the same table. — 抱怨的細節

I believe we are entitled to receive compensation for the poor food quality and services. I expect you to pay us the equivalent amount of the meal as compensation.

I look forward to receiving your cheque for this amount within the next 14 days. — 賠償的要求

Yours faithfully,
Carmen Pliego

敬啟者：

我寫信來投訴上週五我和我丈夫到貴餐廳用餐時，所受到的待遇令人無法接受。

首先，儘管我們已經事先訂位，我們被安排到洗手間正前方的座位，因為當時沒有別的桌位。第二，我們等了快半小時才有人送菜過來。更糟的是，我們點的牛排煎過頭，而沙拉居然是溫的。還有，我們被迫9點就要離開，因為有別人訂了這桌位子。

我相信我們有權就你們糟糕的餐點品質和服務要求補償。我希望你們能賠償與當日餐點等值的金額。

期望能在接下來14天內，收到上述金額的支票。

Carmen Pliego 敬上

情境三　抱怨新買的智慧型手機又出問題了

寫作技巧錦囊

Who are you writing to?　寫給誰？
→ mobile phone shop / retailer

What do you complain about?　抱怨什麼？
→ report on defects / imperfection / problems of the phone / poor customer / after-sales service

Details of the **complaint**　抱怨的細節
→ problems

What do you ask the phone provider to do?　你要店員做什麼？
→ exchange / replace with a new one / test and repair / refund

單字片語搶先看

1. **faulty** *adj.* 故障的；有問題的；功能有瑕疵的
   - Customers may ask for a refund if the purchased items are faulty.
     如果購買的物品有問題，顧客可以要求退費。

2. **brand new** *adj.* 全新的 ⟷ used, second-hand
   - Many customers flocked into this brand new shopping mall.
     很多顧客湧入這棟全新的購物商場。

3. **work** *vi. vt.* 功能正常運作；使工作 ⟷ malfunction
   - The mailing function of the cell phone isn't working. I can't edit text messages.
     這隻手機的發信功能有問題。我沒辦法編寫簡訊。

4. **monitor** *n.[C]* 螢幕 *(=screen, display)*
   - I dropped my phone by accident and the monitor shattered into pieces.
     我不小心讓手機掉到地上，螢幕碎成碎片。

5. **model** *n.[C]* 機型
   - The tablet manufacturer just launched its latest model.
     這個平板電腦製造商剛推出一款最新的機型。

6. **warranty** *n.[C]* 保固期
   - The mobile retailer repaired my cell phone free of charge because it's under warranty.
     手機零售商幫我免費修理手機，因為它還在保固期內。
   - under warranty 在保固期內

7. **malfunction** *vi. n.* 發生故障；故障
   - A warning light seems to have malfunctioned.
     一盞警示燈似乎故障了。

英文範例

【★可替換其他抱怨細節】

抱怨新手機的故障問題與售後服務不週到

Dear Sir / Madam,

I am writing to complain about the faulty smartphone that · 對象
I have purchased in your store.

I am Chris Lee, a regular customer of your company.
On the 10th of March, I bought a brand-new Nokia XYZ
mobile. ★ However, upon one week of using it, problems
started to appear. The flash of the camera was no longer
working. Also, the monitor is getting blurry, which makes
it difficult for me to read the SMS messages clearly. I was
very surprised to discover so many problems in quite an
expensive model.

Naturally, since the phone is still under warranty, I returned
it in your store to be replaced with a new one. One of your
sales staff told me that they the new model would be sent
to my home address within one week. However, I got it
THREE weeks later, and the camera of the new phone
malfunctions, too. I am very upset with your poor service
and the poor quality of the phone.

· 抱怨的細節

In this regard, I insist on getting a refund of my full
payment. Please contact me to settle this matter.

· 你想要店員做的事

Yours faithfully,
Chris Lee

段落大意

寫信目的	開場可直接點名是來抱怨，或先說自己原本有很高期待，但卻得到令人失望的產品或服務。
問題核心	以陳述事實的口吻，點出產品的瑕疵。
敬請回覆	要求對方退換貨 / 退款 / 修理，或純粹要求對方下次要改進。
信尾	客套語 + 署名。

中文翻譯

您好：

我寫信來抱怨我在你們店裡的智慧型手機故障了。3月時我在你們店裡買了一支全新的Nokia XYZ手機，然而才剛用了一個禮拜，就開始出現問題，相機的閃光燈故障了。此外，螢幕顯示變得很模糊，讓我很難看清楚簡訊，我很訝異居然這麼貴的手機有這麼多毛病。

既然手機還在保固期內，很自然的我當時就把它拿到你們店裡要換支新機。其中一位銷售人員告訴我新機一個禮拜內就會送到我家。但後來拖了三個禮拜才拿到，而且新手機的相機功能還是故障。我很不滿意你們的售後服務以及手機的品質。

考慮上述因素，我堅持要全額退費。請與我聯繫處理這個問題。

Chris 李　敬上

換個對象寫寫看

手機設計上的瑕疵

- The battery of this model runs out so quickly. So whenever I browse Facebook, listen to a few tunes and send an email or two, suddenly I am in the red! Also, I constantly suffer poor signal. What makes matters worse, as I load more apps and music on to it, the response time for loading and calling is getting much slower, which is really annoying!

  這種機型的手機電池消耗很快。所以每當我瀏覽臉書，聽幾首曲子，寄一兩封email，電池就會突然地快耗盡了。此外，我常有通訊不良的問題。更糟的是，隨著我下載更多應用程式和音樂，下載速度和發話反應變得越來越慢，這真是令人生氣！

售後服務與維修問題

- I dialed the customer service toll-free hotline and spoke to someone overseas that did not speak English very well. I could tell by the sound of the connection that it was outsourced to another country. They then transferred my call to the Texas main office. The lady on the phone was very rude and showed no intention to help me with my problem. I told her I needed to talk to a supervisor regarding a phone problem. She gave me a different phone number to call. The manager who spoke to me just told me to send my phone to their technician and they would check. I felt very disappointed about how the company handles problems.

  我撥打客服免付費電話，跟一位英文不好的服務人員說上話，我可以從電話轉接的聲音聽出來他們把客服外包到另一個國家來處理。接著我的電話被轉接到德州總公司，接電話的女士口氣很不好，也沒有想要解決問題的意思，我跟她說我要和她的主管陳述我手機故障的事，她就叫我撥另一支電話號碼。跟我說話的經理只說要我把我的故障手機寄去他們的維修部門作檢查，該公司處理手機問題的方法讓我很失望。

其他抱怨信常見的萬用語

- I hope you can take this matter seriously and take effective measures to solve the issue.

  我希望你們能認真看待此事並採取有效的措施解決問題。

- I think I'm entitled for either a replacement or a full refund.

  我認為我有權要求換新機或全額退費。

句型解說在這裡

句型 1

> S + make it +adj. + for O + to V　　……讓……做一件事變得……

- The noise made it difficult for us to sleep well.
  噪音讓我們很難入睡。

延伸觀念

it當虛主詞或虛受詞

> It is adj. to V (it指的就是to V)　　做一件事是……的

- It is impossible to get this job done in two days.
  要在兩天內把這工作完成是不可能的。

> It takes sb time to V　　人做一件事要花多少時間

- It took me 2 hours to finish the report.
  我花了2小時寫完這篇報告。

> make it adj. to V

- The Internet makes it convenient for people around the world to contact each other.
  網路讓世界各地的人能更便利的彼此聯絡。

句型2

> insist on + N / Ving　　堅持

- I insist on getting a replacement for my faulty phone.
  我堅持我故障的手機要換新機。
- = I insist on a replacement for my faulty phone.

延伸觀念

> insist on + N / V-ing

- I insist on getting a full refund for my purchase.
  我堅持我購買的品項要全額退費。
  = I insist on a full refund for my purchase.

> insist (that) + S + (should) +VR

- I insist (that) a full refund (should) be made.
  我堅持要全額退費。

練習時間試試看

抱怨手機故障

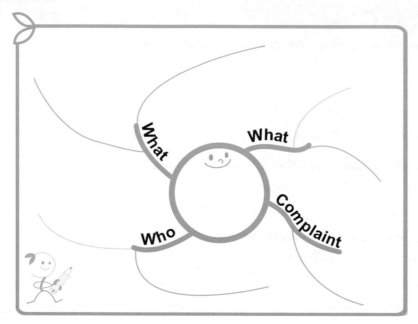

 Who are you writing to? 對象？

 What do you complain about? 抱怨什麼

 Details of the **complaint** 抱怨的細節

 What do you ask the phone provider to do?
你想要手機供應商做什麼

練習範例分享

Dear Sir / Madam,　　　　　　　　　　　　　　　　　　　　對象

I am Ted Chou, and I'm writing to complain about the
faulty i-Phone 4S that I purchased in your store on
Sept 9th.

Upon two weeks of using the brand new cell phone,
I had problems of poor signal. I could talk for about a
minute, sometimes shorter, and then the other person
couldn't hear me. I brought my phone in to Apple 4
to 5 times for testing, only to find the reception of the
sales staff was horrible and offered no help. When they
finally replaced it with a new one, the same problem
appears on my new phone, which is very disappointing!　　抱怨的細節

I want to be compensated for this matter. I'd like to
ask for a full refund and please contact me as soon as　　想要手機供應商
possible to discuss this matter.　　　　　　　　　　　　　　做什麼

Sincerely,
Ted Chou

您好：

我是Ted周，寫信來抱怨我在9月9日跟你購買的i-phone 4S。
我才剛用兩個禮拜就遇到通訊不良的問題。我可以講個大約一分或甚至不到一分
鐘，對方就聽不到我的聲音。我把手機送去蘋果的服務處作了4、5次檢查，只得到
接待人員糟糕的對待，而且他們沒幫上忙。當他們最後終於換新機給我時，同樣的
問題又出現了，這讓我非常失望！

我想針對上述事項索賠，我要求全額退費。請盡速聯絡我討論相關事宜。

Ted 周　敬上

Unit 4

網購

情境一
寫信詢問貨物
配送時間

情境二
更改付費方式

情境三
商品尺寸不合，
詢問換貨

情境一　寫信詢問貨物配送時間

心智圖解說

寫作技巧錦囊

Who are you writing to?　對象？
→ Help Center Best Buy

What do you want to know?　你想知道什麼？
→ When will my order ship? When will my order arrive?

Details of your order　訂單細節
→ name of items / special requirements

單字片語搶先看

1. **order** *n.[C]* 訂單
   - I just placed an online order for office supply and the purchase amount totals $20,000.
     我才剛下了網路訂單訂購辦公室用品，訂單金額合計2萬元。
     詞類變化：order *vi. vt.* 定購

2. **track** *vi. vt.* 追蹤
   - The police have been tracking the four criminals all over central Taiwan.
     警方一直在整個中台灣追查這四名罪犯的下落。

3. **goods** *n.* 商品 *(=product, merchandise)*
   - There is a large discrepancy between the description of the goods and what I got.
     商品描述和我實際買到的東西有很大的落差。

4. **freshly-baked** *adj.* 剛出爐的
   - Customers line up for the freshly-baked baguettes and croissants.
     顧客排隊為了搶買剛出爐的法式長棍麵包和可頌麵包。

5. **bouquet** *n.[C]* 花束
   - We brought our mom a bouquet of carnations on Mother's Day.
     我們在母親節當天買給媽媽一束花。

6. **shipping** *n.[U]* 運輸
   - shipping fee運費
   - If items are cancelled from an order and the order total falls below the minimum purchase amount for free shipping, then a shipping and handling fee will be applied to the remaining items.
     如果刪除訂單上某些品項，導致訂單總金額低於免運費的門檻，則運費和手續費會被加在剩下的品項上。

7. **residential** *adj.* 住宅的
   - The residential area and the commercial area are mixed in most cities in Taiwan.
     台灣大多數城市裡住宅區和商業區是混合的。
     詞類變化：reside *vi.* 居住　resident *n.[C]* 居民

英文範例

【★可替換其他疑問】

請對方以急件在24小時內送貨到府

Dear Sir / Ma'am,   ● 對象

My membership number is A02515. I am writing this

letter to inquire the delivery status of my online order,

tracking number Z1021.

★ I placed the order this morning and the goods

included:

A freshly-baked chocolate birthday cake

A bouquet of 99 roses

I selected urgent delivery and I paid an extra 150NT for

shipping.

I expect the order to arrive at my residential address

within 1 business day.   ● 訂單細節

I hope you can process my order promptly and reply to

this inquiry a.s.a.p.

Thanks for your time.

Yours truthfully,

Jack Tseng

段落大意

寫信目的 開場可直接說明你在何時訂購商品,想詢問配送時間。

商品或配送細節 提醒對方你訂的商品內容或配送上的要求。

敬請回覆 要求對方回覆確認。

信尾 客套語 + 署名。

中文翻譯

您好:

我的會員代號是A02515。我寫信的目的是要詢問我的網路訂單寄送狀態。訂單代號是Z1021。

我在今早訂的品項包含:
一個現做巧克力生日蛋糕
一束99朵玫瑰花束
我選擇急件快遞,也已額外付了150元的運費。
我希望貨品能在一個工作天內送達我的住家地址。

希望您能盡速處理我的訂單並回覆以上詢問。

謝謝您的時間。

Jack 曾 敬上

換個對象寫寫看

【★可替換其他疑問】

詢問能否週六日送貨

- I'd like to know more about your delivery policy. Once I place my order, can I ask it to be delivered on Saturdays or Sundays to places in Taipei City? Are you able to do Saturday or Sunday deliveries?
  我想要知道更多關於你們的送貨規定。一旦我下了訂單,我可以要求你們週六或週日運送到台北市內的地方嗎?你們是否接受週六日送件?

送貨時收件者不在家該如何處理?

- The customer service staff says your couriers deliver between 9.30am and 5.30pm. If I am not home when you attempt to deliver, what will you do? Will the courier leave you a calling card so I can rearrange the delivery for a more convenient day?
  客服人員告訴我你們的送貨時間是早上9點半到下午5點半。如果你們要送貨時我不在家,你們會如何處理?送貨員會留給我他的名片,讓我跟他聯繫安排其他方便收件的日期嗎?

其他常見的網路購物疑問

1. How can I check the information / ratings and reviews of the merchant / seller / retailer / store?
   我如何事先查看商人／賣家／零售商／商店的資料與評價?
2. What is the minimum purchase amount for free shipping?
   要消費多少金額才能免運費?
3. Will the merchant ship outside Taipei City?
   賣家是否可以送貨到台北以外的縣市?
4. I'd like to select my work address instead of my home address for billing and for shipping my purchases. How can I change / alter my billing and shipping information?
   我想把帳單和送貨地址從住家改成我的公司地址。我該如何更改帳單地址或送貨地址?

句型解說在這裡

句型1

place an order　　下訂單

⌐ It's easy to place an online order if you are already a member of this website.
若你已經是該網站的會員，在網路上下訂單很簡單。

延伸觀念

place an order 下訂單；place an bid競標；place an emphasis on... 強調
⌐ Online shoppers can choose either to place a bid or purchase the item at a fixed price.
網路買家可以選擇下標競價或是以定價購買商品。

句型2

S + include + O　　包含

⌐ The items I have purchased on the website include accessories and cosmetics.
我在這網站上以購買過的商品包含飾品和化妝品。

延伸觀念

include *vt.* including *adj.*，included *adj* 的用法：

1. include 前面接S（名詞）
   ⌐ The nominees for Nobel Peace Prize include several workers for non-profit organizations.
   諾貝爾和平獎的被提名人包含了好幾位非營利組織的工作人員。
2. including 為which include(s)的分詞片語，前接接句子和逗點，後面接名詞
   ⌐ Many people are nomineed for the Nobel Peace Prize, including several NPOs workers / which includes several NPO workers.

3. included為and ... is included的分詞片語，前接接句子和逗點，名詞則放在前面
   ⌐ Many people are nomineed for the Nobel Peace Prize, several workers for NPOs included and several NPO workers are included.

練習時間試試看

詢問可否更改送貨地址

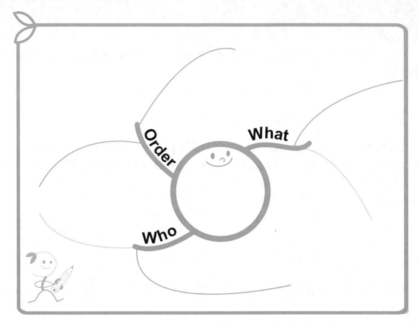

 Who are you writing to? 對象？

 What do you want to know? 你想知道什麼？

 Details of your **order** 訂單細節

練習範例分享

Dear Sir / Ma'am,

My membership number is ZU3021. I am writing this
letter to change the current recipient address for my
order, tracking number PA2100.

I've checked the delivery status of the order with your
staff and I've been informed it'll arrive before noon
tomorrow. But since I won't be home to receive it, I'd
like to get the order shipped to my work address as
follows:

8F, No 32, Sec 3, Min-Chuang West Road, Taipei City

Please reply for confirmation of the above request.
Thanks for your time.

Yours truthfully,

Ben Ten

對象

為什麼想換
收貨地址？

你想要對方
做什麼

您好：

我的會員代號是ZU3021，我寫信目的要更改我的送貨地址，訂單代號是PA2100。
我剛和你們的人員查詢了目前送貨狀態，我被告知商品會在中午前送達。但因為我
到時候不會在家，我想要本筆訂單改送到我的公司地址，地址如下：

台北市民權西路三段32號8樓

請回信確認收到以上要求。
謝謝您的時間。

Ben Ten　敬上

情境二　更改付費方式

心智圖解說

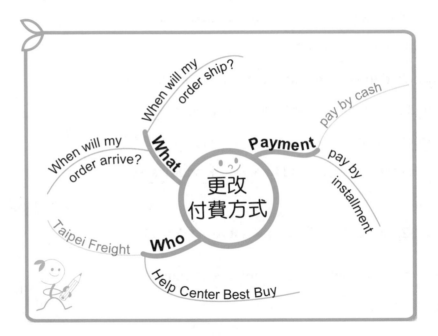

When will my order ship?

When will my order arrive?

What

pay by cash

Payment

pay by installment

Taipei Freight

Who

更改
付費方式

Help Center Best Buy

寫作技巧錦囊

Step 1　Who are you writing to?　對象？
→ Help Center Best Buy

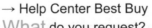
Step 2　What do you request?　要求什麼？
→ When will my order ship? When will my order arrive?

Step 3　Payment option　付款選項
→ pay by installment

單字片語搶先看

1. method　*n.[C]* 方式 (= way)
   - An experienced teacher must master teaching methods.
     一位經驗豐富的老師一定專精於教學方法。

2. cash on delivery　貨到付款
   - Most customers without any bank account can choose to pay cash on deliver.
     大部分沒有銀行帳號的顧客可以選擇貨到付款。

3. tablet　*n.[C]* 平板電腦
   - This computer manufacturer just launched its latest model of tablets.
     這家電腦製造商剛推出一款平板電腦。
     延伸字彙：桌上電腦 desktop　筆記型電腦 laptop

4. installment　*n.[C]* 分期付款
   - I'd like to pay for the jewelry by 6 installments.
     我想以6期分期付款購買珠寶。

5. interest　*n.[C]* 利息；興趣
   - The interest rate for mortgage is rising increasingly over the years.
     貸款利率這幾年來不斷上升。

6. spread　*vi. vt.* 分散；使延展 (=divide)
   - The bills are sent out on different dates to spread the workload on council staff.
     這些法案分不同日期寄送，以分攤委員會的工作負擔。

7. tax　*n.[C,U]* 稅；稅金
   - He already pays 40% tax on his income.
     他的收入的4成都已拿去納稅。

英文範例

【★可替換其他付費方式】

訂單更換其他付費方式

Dear Sir,

I am writing to change the payment method for my · 對象

latest order, Tracking Number TF2351.

★Instead of paying cash on delivery for the tablet, I'd

like to pay by 4 installments by credit card with 0%

interest. · 你要求什麼

I just noticed from your website about Pay Easy

Installment Plan. It says that customers can spread the

total purchase amount over several monthly payments

with no interest. (Shipping and taxes will be added to the

first payment.) The total value of my order is $399, so I

will be charged with 4 monthly payments to my visa. · 付款選項

Please reply for confirmation of the above request.

Sincerely,

Julie Tseng

段落大意

寫信目的 開場先給予訂單資料，並直接說明要更改付費方式。

細節 更改付費方式的細節。

敬請回覆 要求對方收到訊息後回覆確認。

信尾 客套語 ＋ 署名。

中文翻譯

先生您好：

我寫信來修改我最近一次的訂單（訂單索引號碼TF2351）。原本我選貨到付款，但我想改成分四期零利率刷卡付款。

我剛從你們網站上得知有關Pay Easy分期付款的方案。規定上說能將付款金額平均分攤成幾個月零利率（運費和貨物稅則會被加在第一期付款金額內）我的訂單總金額為399美金，所以你們會以四期零利率向我的信用卡扣款。

請回覆確認以上要求。

Julie 曾　敬上

換個對象寫寫看

選擇貨到付款

Since I don't want to make credit card payments, I prefer cash on delivery payment. When I receive the goods, your staff can collect the payment for the item right away .

因為我不想要信用卡付款，我想要選擇貨到付款。當我收到貨品時，您的送貨員就可以立刻向我收款。

變更信用卡內容

I'd like to switch from Visa to Master Card.
Card Holder's Name: Jeremy C. Chen
Card number: 4851 5214 9635 7458
Expiring Date 2015 / 04 / 23
security number (the last 3 digits on reverse of card) 351
Please confirm receiving the updated credit card details.

我想從visa卡改成萬事達卡。

持卡人姓名Jeremy C. Chen
卡號4851 5214 9635 7458
失效日期 2015年4月23日
認證號碼(卡片背後末三碼351)

請確認收到以上更新後的信用卡資訊

其他更改付費方式常見的萬用語

1. I'd like to alter my payment options from paying by cash to telegraphic transfer.
   我想要將付款選擇從現金付款改為電匯。

2. I'm writing this email to alter / update my payment method. I'd like to pay by when the shipment is ready.
   我寫信來更改／更新我的付費方式。我想要等貨物準備好後再電匯。

3. Please kindly help with my request for change of payment terms.
   煩請協助我變更付款方式。

4. I'd like to request to update my payment method. I will go with paying by check.
   我想要求變更付款方式。我會以支票付款。

句型解說在這裡

句型1

instead of + N / V-ing　　而不是

- Since it is still raining outside, let's stay home instead of going outside.
  既然還在下雨，我們待在家好了，不要外出。
- You probably picked up my keys instead of yours.
  你可能拿了我的鑰匙，而不是你自己的。

延伸觀念

比較instead和instead of

1. instead of：後面接的「N / V-ing」是主詞沒有去做的事。
   - Many young people download songs instead of purchasing CDs.
     很多年輕人下載音樂而不買CD。
2. instead：前面接否定句子代表主詞沒做的選擇。後面先逗點，再接句子，代表主詞真正的選擇。
   - Many young people don't buy CDs anymore. Instead, they download music.

句型2

It (告示牌，規定) says that +子句　　規定上寫說……

- The refund policy says that I can get a full refund for defective products under warranty.
  退費規定上寫說，我可以對還在保固期內的瑕疵商品要求全額退費。

延伸句型

It is said that + 名詞子句　　據說……

- It is said that this millionaire has devoted 80% of his fortune to charities.
  據說這位百萬富翁已經將八成財產捐給了慈善團體。

練習時間試試看

要求更改付費方式：從貨到付款改為ATM轉帳

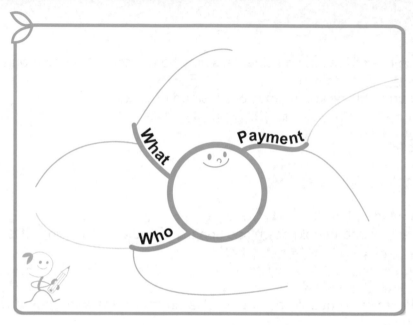

 Step 1 Who are you writing to?　對象？

 Step 2 What do you request?　要求什麼？

 Step 3 Payment option　付款選項

練習範例分享

Dear Sir,

I am writing to change the payment method for my

latest order, Tracking Number BM3521.

I'd like to choose ATM transactions for the amount of

the order, instead of cash on delivery.

Since this order has exceeded 400 dollars, it's

inconvenient for me to withdraw that much money

in cash from my bank account. I will transfer the

total amount to your account no later than 2:00 pm

tomorrow.

Please reply for confirmation of the above request.

Sincerely,

Mandy Chou

對象

要求什麼

付款選項

您好：

我寫信來修改我最近一次的訂單的付款方式（訂單索引號碼BM3521）。原本我選貨到付款，但我想改成ATM轉帳。

因為訂單金額超過400美元，要我從帳戶提領那麼多現金其實很不方便。我會在明天下午兩點前將總金額匯到你的帳戶。

請回覆確認以上要求。

Mandy 邱 敬上

情境三　商品尺寸不合，詢問換貨

心智圖解說

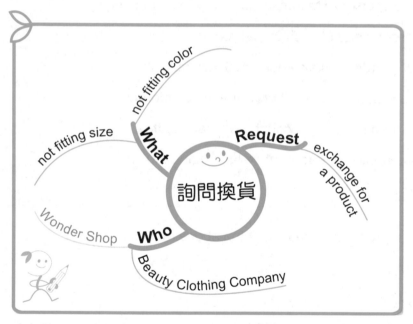

寫作技巧錦囊

Who are you writing to?　對象？
→ customer service, Beauty Clothing Company

What do you request?　要求什麼？
→ exchange for a product

Why do you ask for exchange of an item?　為什麼要換貨？
→ not fitting (size): too large / small / tight / loose / long / short

單字片語搶先看

1. **trousers** *n.[C]* 褲子 (= pants)
   - He just spent NT$399 for a pair of designer jeans. What a bargain!
     他只花了399元就買到一條設計師款的牛仔褲。真是撿到便宜！

2. **mail order** 郵購
   - She buys cosmetics and skin care products by mail order once a month.
     她每個月用郵購方式買化妝品和護膚產品。

3. **waist** *n.[C]* 腰部
   - The skirt was too big around the waist.
     這件裙子在腰部的地方太寬大。

4. **length** *n.[C,U]* 長度
   - This ankle-length dress looks nice on Mary.
     這件長度到腳踝的洋裝穿在Mary身上很好看。

5. **unfortunately** *adv.* 不幸地；很遺憾地
   - We tried to ask you out to go shopping. Unfortunately, you were out of town when we called.
     我們原本想邀請你出來一起購物。但遺憾的是，當我們打電話時，你人已經出城了。

6. **parcel** *n.[C]* 包裹 (= package)
   - The parcel was delivered last week and the recipient got it this morning.
     這個包裹上週寄出，收件人今早拿到。

7. **invoice** *n.[C]* 發票；發貨單
   - Enclosed the package please find the invoice of all the items of this order.
     包裹內附上這次訂購的所有物品的發票。

英文範例

【★可替換其他換貨原因和要求】

訂單更換其他付費方式

Dear Customer Service,

對象

I am writing to ask for an exchange for the pair of linen trousers I recently purchased by mail order, Order Number TF2351. ★The pants included with this order are a 28 waist with a 34 length. Unfortunately I need to exchange these for the same pants with a size of 24 waist and 32 length.

要求什麼

想換貨的原因

Please send someone to pick up the parcel. I'll enclose with this item a copy of the invoice and order number. I also understand there are no shipping charges added for making an exchange.

If you could please send the exchanged item to my home address, I would appreciate it.

Sincerely,

Isabella Freed

段落大意

寫信目的	開場先給予訂單資料，並直接說明要求換貨。
細節	換貨原因和想要換的商品條件說明。
敬請回覆	要求對方收到訊息後回覆確認。
信尾	客套語 + 署名。

中文翻譯

客服人員您好：

我寫信來要求更換我以郵購買的尼龍褲（訂單索引號碼TF2351）。我訂單上買的褲子是腰圍28吋、長34吋。但很遺憾的我需要更換成腰圍24吋長、32吋的同款式褲子。

請派人來收回包裹，我會附上發票影本和訂單編號。我瞭解我不必為換貨負擔運費。

若你們能將更換的商品送到我的住家地址，我將不勝感激。

Isabella Freed　敬上

換個對象寫寫看

商品描述和實際收到的不符

⊙ I'd like to exchange the backpack I purchased for a handbag of the same design. There is a large discrepancy between how the backpack is described and what I received. It was described as light-weight with lots of functional layers to hold a variety of items. But when I got it, I found it heavier than I expected and there are only three layers inside. I'd like to exchange for the handbag because it will be more useful to me.

我想要把我買的背包換成同款式的手提包。我拿到的背包和它當初的描述差很多。商品描述上寫說它重量很輕，有很多夾層可以擺放不同種類的東西。但實際拿到時，我發現它比我預期來的重，且裡面只有三個夾層。我想要換同款手提包，因為比較實用。

因外觀和顏色而換貨

⊙ I'd like to exchange the pink skirt for the light-blue one of the same pattern. When I first saw the pink one on your TV shopping channel, the color seemed bright and rich. But when I received it, I am not very into the color because it's fading pink. Please send me the light-blue skirt.

我想把這件粉紅色裙子換成同花樣的淡藍色裙。當我在電視購物頻道上看到粉紅色裙時，我覺得它的色彩很亮很飽和。但當我拿到時，粉紅色看起來像褪色，我不是很喜歡。請換成淺藍色的。

其他要求換貨常見的萬用語

1. The size 8 jeans don't fit well. They're good for my waist but too tight through the thighs and butt. I'd like to exchange for a size 10.
   這件8號尺碼的牛仔褲不合身，雖然腰部剛好，但大腿到臀部的部分對我來說太緊。我想要換成10號尺碼。
2. I've found the size 23 shoes unfit. They are too tight for me. I'd like to exchange for size 24.
   我發現這雙23號的鞋子不合腳，他們太緊了，我想換成24號。

句型解說在這裡

句型1

exchange (n / v) for......　　換成……

1. exchange A for B 把A換成B
   - May I exchange the blue T-shirt for a purple one?
     我可以把藍色的T恤換成紫色的嗎？
2. exchange for B 換成B
   - This bank deals with exchange for foreign currencies.
     這家銀行可處理外幣兌換。

句型2

There be +名詞 + V-ing / p.p.　　有……在做／被……

- There are a lot of workers from this company going on a strike.
  有很多該公司的員工走上街頭罷工。
- There is a cat run over by a car on the highway.
  高速公路上有一隻被車子輾過的貓。

延伸觀念

　名詞後面的which / who關係子句，可以省略關係代名詞who / which，
　後面的動詞改為分詞（主動語態改為V-ing；被動語態改為p.p.）
- There are two boys playing in the playground.
  有兩個男生正在操場上玩遊戲。
  = There are two boys who are playing....（主動語態）
- There was a lot of trash littered on the ground. 地上被丟滿了垃圾。
  = There was a lot of trash which was littered....（被動語態）

練習時間試試看

要求換貨： 褲子不合身

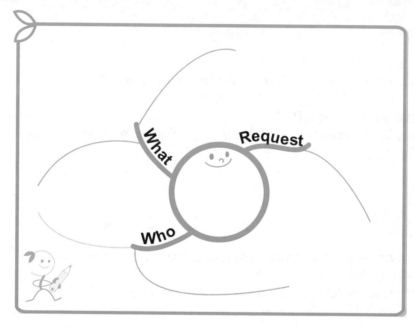

 Who are you writing to? 對象？

 What do you **request**? 要求什麼？

 What do you ask for exchange of an item? 為什麼要換貨？

練習範例分享

Dear Customer Service,　　　　　　　　　　　　　　● 對象

I am writing to ask for an exchange for the pair of low

rise jeans I recently purchased, Order Number 255121.　● 要求什麼

I like the color, cut, and the texture. Yet they don't fit me

properly. The size 10 jeans are too loose on the waist

and on the butt. That makes my bum look big on them!

I hope I can get a smaller size on return from your

wonderful and well stocked store at your earliest

convenience.　　　　　　　　　　　　　　　● 想換貨的原因

Sincerely,

Belle Tan

客服人員您好：

我寫信來要求更換我買的低腰牛仔褲（訂單索引號碼255121）。

我喜歡它的顏色、剪裁還有質感，但對我來說不合身，這件10號尺碼的牛仔褲在腰圍和臀部的部分都太鬆了，這讓我穿起來屁股看起來很大。

希望能盡速從你們款式齊全的店裡，取得一件小尺碼的牛仔褲。

Belle譚　敬上

Unit 5

學校

情境一
小組報告彙整

情境二
請教授寫推薦信

情境三
詢問留學課程

情境一　小組報告彙整

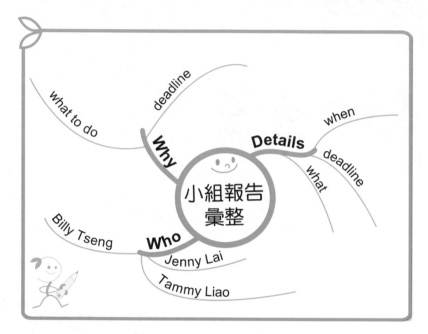

寫作技巧錦囊

Who are you writing to?　寫給誰？
→ Tammy Liao, Jenny Lai, Bill Tseng

Why do you write this email?　為什麼要寫這封電子郵件？
→ to remind them what to do and the deadline of their report

Details of your email　電子郵件的細節
→ deadline / when / what

單字片語搶先看

1. panel discussion 小組討論
   - The panel discussion ran well because each member contributed a lot and did their fair share.
   小組討論進行得很順利，因為每位成員都貢獻很多，且平均分擔工作。
   相關字詞：study group讀書會

2. participant *n.[C]* 與會者；參與者
   - The participants of the meeting came well-prepared so the discussion went smoothly.
   會議的與會者都有充分準備，所以討論進行的很順利。
   詞類變化：participate *vi. vt.* 參加；分享

3. convener *n.[C]* 召集人
   - This convener of the group project encourages members to interact cooperatively.
   這個小組計畫的召集人鼓勵所有成員彼此合作互動。
   相關字詞：聯絡人liaison

4. deadline *n.[C]* 截止日期 *(= due time)*
   - The team members are working under pressure to meet the deadline for submission of the report.
   這個小組的成員在時間壓力下工作，為了要在截止日前交出報告。

5. submit *vi. vt.* 忍受；繳交
   - Every day before class starts we all need to submit the assignments for the previous class.
   每天上課前我們都要繳交前一次上課的作業。
   詞類變化：submission *n.[C]* 繳交（物）

6. assign *vt.* 分配；指派 *(=delegate)*
   - A good supervisor doesn't necessarily assign the most challenging task to the most capable worker.
   一個好的主管不見得會把最有挑戰性的工作指派給最有能力的人。

7. revision *n.[C,U]* 修訂；校訂；修正
   - This rough draft of report still needs a lot of editing and revision.
   這個報告的草稿需要大量的編輯與修改。
   詞類變化：revise *vi. vt.* 修訂；校訂

英文範例

請小組討論成員在本週email各自負責的報告內容給你

【★可替換其他需要小組成員合作的事項】

Dear Panel Discussion Participants, 　　　　　　　　　　　對象

As a convener, I would like to kindly remind you that

the deadline for our group report to Professor Charlotte

Tsai is next Friday November 4th. 　　　　　　　　　　　為什麼

★ Please submit to me the parts you are assigned by

this Friday, October 28th at 10 pm. In this way, I can

put the separate reports together and look over them.

So all of us can proofread, and discuss for revision at

our meeting next Monday at 4:00 pm in the Student

Lounge. 　　　　　　　　　　　　　　　　　　　　　　細節

Your cooperation will be much appreciated.

Regards,
Dan Dove

段落大意

寫信目的 開場可直接說明繳交報告的截止日期。

細節 提醒對方和交報告相關的注意事項。

敬請回覆 要求對方回覆確認。

信尾 客套語 + 署名。

中文翻譯

小組討論的成員們大家好：

身為召集人，我想提醒每位組員：我們要在下週五（11月4日）前繳交我們的小組報告給Charlotte蔡教授。

請在本週五（10月28日）晚上10點前，將你們各自分配到的報告內容寄給我。這樣一來，我可以利用週末將報告彙整並核對。我們就可以在下週一下午4點，在學生休息室舉辦的小組討論會上校對內容並且討論修改方向。

感謝大家的配合。

Dan Dove 敬上

換個對象寫寫看

提醒每個人分配要蒐集資料並完成的內容

⊙ As is mentioned in class, the topic of our joint report is _____. And please consider how you may contribute to the group effort by gathering research information and writing a 500-word report on one of the following subtopics. Please reply this email by tomorrow 10:00 am and let me know which subtopic you would like to be assigned. If more than two members volunteer for the same part or if any of these subtopic isn't covered, I'll delegate assign the tasks.

如同課堂上所提到的，我們分組報告的主題是⋯⋯。請大家思考如何能貢獻所學，每個人可以選擇以下其一子題，蒐集資訊並寫成500字報告。請在明天早上10點前回信，讓我知道你想被分配哪個子題。如果2人以上想負責相同子題，或有子題沒人認領，我會負責分配。

要開會討論如何分配上台簡報

⊙ Our joint presentation topic is _____. And our presentation time is Next Tuesday at 10:00am. I'd like to receive your individual presentation in PowerPoint format by this Wednesday. And I also hope to schedule a meeting time this Friday afternoon at around 3:00pm to discuss about the content details and the rundown, and then rehearse the presentation. Please reply this email by midnight tonight and let me know if you are available for the rehearsal time.

我們的聯合簡報主題是⋯⋯，上台報告時間是下週二早上10點。我希望能在本週三前收到你們個別的簡報的PowerPoint檔案。我也希望我們能在本週五下午約3點左右開個會，討論內容細節以及流程，並且演練簡報過程。請在今晚午夜前回信告訴我是否能配合開會時間。

句型解說在這裡

句型1

remind O +	that 子句	提醒……
	of + 名詞	

- I'm writing this email to remind you that the assignment is due this Friday.
  我寫這封信用來提醒你作業要在本週五前交。
- Parents always remind their children of the danger of playing in the kitchen.
  父母總是提醒孩子在廚房玩耍的危險性。

延伸觀念

remind 受詞 (not) to V：提醒某人（不）要去做

- Parents always remind their children not to play in the kitchen.
  父母總是提醒孩子不要在廚房玩。

句型2

可分開的動詞片語	動詞片語＋一般受詞（非代名詞）＝一般受詞（非代名詞）放在動詞片語中間 - The convener is in charge of putting together <u>the individual reports</u>. = The convener is in charge of putting <u>the individual reports</u> together. 召集人要負責整合個別的報告內容。
	若受詞為代名詞(me, you, them, him, her, it, us)，一定要放在動詞片語中間 - The convener is in charge to put <u>them</u> together.
不可分開的動詞片語	不管受詞是一般名詞或代名詞，都放在動詞片語之後 - The convener is in charge to look over the individual reports / them.

練習時間 試試看

詢問大家看完彙整後的小組報告的想法

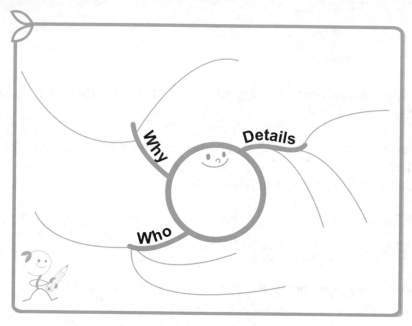

 Who are you writing to?　對象？

 Why do you write this email?　為什麼？

 Details of your email　細節？

練習範例分享

Dear Panel Discussion Participants,　　　　　　　• 對象

Thanks for your efforts in contributing your ideas to the
joint report. As a convener, I have revised the report
several times based on your feedback and attached
the latest version to this email. Please read through the
attached file thoroughly, so we can exchange ideas at
next Monday's meeting at the Brown's Café at 4:00 pm.　• 為什麼

Our deadline for submitting the report is next Thursday.
I'd like to have a meeting by this weekend to go through
the report for a final version. Since we will all attend
Professor Tsai's lecture this Wednesday, I propose we
have a meeting in the lecture room right after the class.
Please let me know if the time is fine with you.　　　　• 細節

Your prompt reply will be very appreciated
Regards,
Ben Jeckings

小組討論的成員們大家好：

謝謝你們投注心力貢獻你的意見，完成小組報告。身為召集人，我已經根據大家的
意見修改內容好幾次，並以附件寄發給大家。請仔細讀過附件，這樣我們就能在下
週一下午4點在Brown咖啡廳舉辦的討論會上交流意見。
我們報告繳交的截止日是下週四。我想要在本週末前和大家開會瀏覽過全部報告內
容，做成最終版本。既然我們本週三都會去聽蔡教授的講課，我建議我們演講完畢
後就在演講室裡開會。請讓我知道這個時間你是否有空。

若您能盡速回覆，將不勝感激。

Ben Jeckings 敬上

情境二　請教授寫推薦信

心智圖解說

寫作技巧錦囊

Who are you writing to?　要寫給誰？
→ Professor Yang

What do you **request**?　你要求什麼？
→ to write a recommendation letter

What school / field do you apply to?　你申請什麼學校？
→ Law School, Princeton University

Why do you apply to this school / program / course?　為什麼要申請？
→ interested in the program: It provides a dual degree program to also receive an MBA

Other details　其他細節
→ admission term, application due

單字片語搶先看

1. **letter of recommendation** 推薦信
   - Try to get letters of recommendation from bosses and colleagues to highlight the strength of your work experience.
   嘗試向老闆或同事取得推薦信，強調你在工作經驗上的強項。
   相關字詞：recommend *vi. vt.* 推薦

2. **contribute** *vi. vt.* 貢獻；捐獻
   - Advance in Technology has contributed to the convenience in communication.
   科技的進步帶來了通訊便利。

3. **development** *n.[C,U]* 生長；進化；發展
   - This country is enjoying thriving economic development.
   這個國家受惠於經濟的蓬勃發展。
   詞類變化：develop *vi. vt.* 進步；使成長

4. **dedication** *n.[U]* 供奉；努力 *(+ to)*
   - A party was held to celebrate the retired worker's dedication to the company.
   為了感謝這名退休員工對公司付出的心力，公司辦了一場派對。
   詞類變化：dedicate *vt.* 以……奉獻

5. **academics** 學業
   - Most people in Asian countries put a lot of emphasis on academics.
   大多數亞洲人重視課業。
   詞類變化：academic *adj.* 學術的

6. **admission** *n.[C,U]* 進入許可；加入許可；入學許可
   - The admission committee evaluate each candidate's academic background .
   入學委員會評估每位申請人的學術背景。
   詞類變化：admit *vi. vt.* 承認；准許進入

7. **dual degree program** 雙學位
   - A dual degree program involves a student's working for two different university degrees in parallel.
   雙學位意指一位學生同時唸兩個不同的學位。

8. **instruction** *n.[U,P]* 教導；教育；用法說明
   - Install the machine according to the manufacturer's instructions.
   請根據製作商的用法說明安裝這台機器。
   詞類變化：instruct *vt.* 指導

英文範例

【★其他可加入的段落】

請教授寫推薦信

Dear Professor Yang,   • 對象

Happy New Year! I hope you had a great night celebrating and that you are enjoying the time off!

I am writing to ask if you would be willing, time permitting, to write a letter of recommendation for me for my application to law schools. At Boston College, your classes   • 要求
were on my favorites list and hugely contributed to my development and growth as an individual. I wanted to ask you first for a letter because I believe you were familiar with my approach and dedication to academics.

I am currently applying to law schools for admission in September 2013. My top choice is the Princeton University.   • 內容
I am particularly interested in doing a dual degree program to also receive an MBA; if I were admitted, I would be   • 為什麼
applying for the dual degree program during my first year of law school. ★
Thank you in advance for your time, and consideration. I also wanted to extend an additional thank you for the time I spent under your instruction.

If you are available to write a recommendation letter, please let me know and I can send you further information. My applications are due by March 22nd.   • 細節
I look forward to hearing from you and I wish you a very Happy New Year!

All the best,
Daniel Liao

段落大意

寒喧	開場先向對方問候。
寫信目的	提出請對方寫推薦函的需求，告知要申請學校和科系。
細節	分多段寫為何找這位教授，想要申請該系所的理由……等讓教授更了解你的細節。
敬請回覆	要求對方收到訊息後回覆確認。
信尾	客套語 ＋ 署名。

中文翻譯

楊教授您好：

新年快樂！祝福您今晚很開心的慶祝新年，同時好好享受新年假期。

我寫這封是想詢問您，如果時間允許的話，有沒有意願協助我撰寫申請法學院的推薦信？在波士頓學院求學時，我很喜歡您的課程，您的課程促使我不斷成長。您是我最先詢問的教授，因為我相信您對於我在學業上的讀書方式和努力很熟悉。

我目前正在申請法學院，預計2013年九月入學。我的首選是普林斯頓大學，我對它結合法學與商學管理碩士的雙學位課程很有興趣。若我能錄取，我會在法學院第一學期提出雙學位申請。

在此先謝謝您撥冗閱讀此信。我想藉此機會再次感謝您在我大學期間給我的教導。

請讓我知道您能否撥空幫我撰寫推薦信，若可以的話我會再給您進一步的訊息。我的申請截止日期是3月22日。

期待收到您的消息，祝您新年快樂!

Daniel 廖　敬上

換個對象寫寫看

讓教授了解推薦信內容需涵蓋的重點

☞ Law schools value letters from professors that can contribute to their evaluation of whether I would be an asset to the school and whether I would have the academic fortitude to withstand the demanding curriculum. Basically, members of the admission committee are looking to get a well-rounded picture of each candidate with specific examples and details.

法學院在審查申請資料時，很重視教授的推薦函，他們會從推薦函中瞭解我將是該學院寶貴的人材，以及瞭解我有沒有求學的韌性，以應付未來繁重的學業。基本上來說，審查委員偏愛申請者提供全方面完整的資料，包含舉例和細節。

讓教授了解你為何想要申請該領域

☞ I have become interested in law school over the past year as a trainee in a law firm. The more I learned through my own conversations with lawyers, the more I became convinced that this was the right path for me. Although I haven't yet decided what type of law I would focus on, I would like to use my education to continue working in the firm.

自從我過去這一年在法律事務所擔任實習生以來，我對於法學院的興趣越來越濃厚。我和律師們聊的越多，就越確信這是我未來想走的路。雖然我還沒有確認要唸哪一種特定領域的法律，我很想藉由我未來求學得到的知識，繼續在法律事務所工作。

其他適合請教授寫推薦信的萬用語

1. 恭維和感謝教授
   I really enjoyed your courses and often go back to my notes and my books. I hope that we will get a chance to meet for tea or coffee if you are available, so I can express my gratitude in person.
   我很喜歡上您的課，現在也常回頭翻閱我當初做的筆記和書本。我希望能有機會請您喝杯茶或咖啡，以親自表達對您的感謝。

2. 讓教授瞭解你為何想申請該學院或領域
   I have always been interested in this field, and have been doing relevant work and thus have had related work experience. I would like to pursue further education so to acquire expertise in the field.
   我一直對這個領域很感興趣，現在從事的也是相關的工作，累積了相關的工作經驗。我想要進一步求學深造，打造自己在該領域的專業。

句型解說在這裡

句型1

> be willing / reluctant / eager / keen to V　　願意／不太願意／急著／迫切去做……

- The alumni of the school is willing to donate money to the school to help build a lab.
  這位校友願意捐助資金給校方蓋一座實驗室。
- The child is reluctant to talk about how he was bullied.
  這個小孩不願意講他被霸凌的經過。
- Everyone is eager to know the result of the relay.
  每個人都急著想知道大隊接力的結果。

延伸片語

> would rather VR1 than VR2　　寧願做 VR1 也不願做 VR2

- These revolutionists would rather die than yield to tyranny.
  這些革命人士寧願死也不願屈服於暴政

句型2

> time permitting　　如果時間允許的話

延伸觀念

獨立分詞構句　S_1 + V_1-ing / V_1-pp..., S_2 + V_2...（或前後互換）
省略連接詞，動詞變分詞－主動 → ing、被動 → p.p.（S_1 與 S_2 為不同的主詞）

- If time (S_1) permits, we (S_2) will stop off in Hong Kong to do some shopping.
  → Time permitting, we will stop off in Hong Kong to do some shopping.
  （刪除附屬連接詞if，連接的句子的主動語態動詞permits要變現在分詞 permitting）
  若時間允許的話，我們可以過境香港去購物。
- There (S_1) were fireworks of all sorts, and each (S_2) was brightly colored.
  → There were fireworks of all sorts, each being brightly colored.
  → There were fireworks of all sorts, each brightly colored.
  這裡有不同種類的煙火，每一種都被塗上鮮豔的色彩。

練習時間試試看

請求主管或老闆寫推薦信

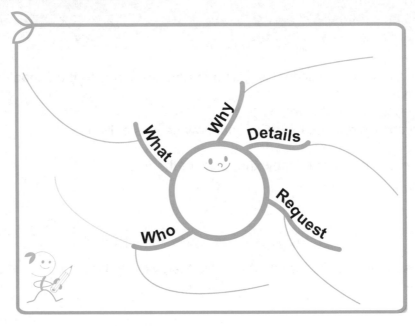

 Step 1　Who are you writing to?　對象？

 Step 2　Who do you reguest?　要求？

 Step 3　What school / field do you apply to ?　內容？

 Step 4　Why do you apply to this school / program / course?　為什麼？

 Step 5　How Other details?　細節？

練習範例分享

Dear Mr. Wang,

First off, Happy Chinese New Year! I hope you are enjoying the holidays!

———————— 對象

I am writing to ask if you could, time-permitting, write a recommendation letter for my application to MBA in Princeton University for September 2013. The more I learned about business management in this company, the more I became convinced that pursuing a degree in MBA would be a good path for me.

———————— 要求
———————— 內容
———————— 為什麼
———————— 細節

I asked you to write this letter because of the respect I have for your work and opinions. As my supervisor, you would be able to write about my analytical, problem-solving and communication skills, as well as my ability to provide high quality service to diverse, global clients, handle heavy work loads, and my potential to be successful in business school and beyond.

I know this is going to be a busy month at work so I understand if it won't be possible to do this - either way, I appreciate your help!

Thank you very much for your help.

Best regards,
Christine Chen

王先生您好：

首先預祝您新年快樂！祝您享受美好的假期！

我寫信是想詢問，若時間許可，您能否幫我寫推薦信，以便我申請2013年秋季入學的普林斯頓大學企管碩士課程。隨著我在這間公司工作期間越來越了解商業管理，我就越確信追求MBA學位是很適合我的途徑。

之所以想請您寫這封推薦信，主要是我十分敬重您的工作專業和意見。身為我的主管，我相信您可以著墨於我的分析、解決問題及溝通的能力，還有我能為不同類型全球各地的客戶提供高品質服務的能力，而且我能應付高工作量，有潛力能在商學院和之後的工作有所成就。

我知道接下來這個月很忙，若您不能撥空撰寫推薦信，我完全能理解。不論如何，我都感謝你的幫忙。

非常謝謝您的幫忙。

Christine 陳 敬上

情境三 詢問留學課程

心智圖解說

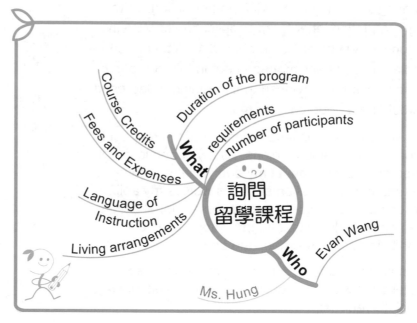

Course Credits
Fees and Expenses
Language of Instruction
Living arrangements

Duration of the program
requirements
number of participants

What

詢問
留學課程

Who

Evan Wang

Ms. Hung

寫作技巧錦囊

Step 1   Who are you writing to? 寫給誰？
→ Evan Wang

Step 2   What do you want to know about? 你想知道什麼？
→ Eligibility requirements and number of participants
Language of Instruction
Duration of the program
Fees and Expenses
Course Credits
Living arrangements

單字片語搶先看

1. apply *vi. vt.* 申請；實施
   - I'm preparing all the academic documents to apply to the law school at Harvard University.
   我正在準備所有學業相關文件以申請哈佛大學法學院。

2. consult *vi. vt.* 商議；諮詢
   - Many international students consult student affairs officers for applying for scholarships.
   很多國際學生會向學生事務處員工詢問如何申請獎學金。

3. international *adj.* 國際的
   - International students consist of 15% of the total number of students in this school.
   國際學生占了這所學校學生總數的百分之15。

4. requirement *n.[C]* 錄取條件
   - What are the GPA and language requirements for admission to the school?
   要入學這所學校的學業成績和語言能力門檻為何？

5. abroad *adv.* 在海外；在國外
   - Only a few undergraduate students at this school consider applying to study abroad programs.
   這所學校只有少數大學生考慮要申請到國外留學的課程。

6. immersion program （為國際學生開的）語言銜接課程
   - This school offers great immersion programs and orientations for international students.
   這所學校為國際學生提供很棒的語言銜接課程和新生訓練。

7. scholarship *n.[C]* 獎學金
   - Only students whose GPA is over 3.0 can apply for scholarships.
   只有學業平均成績超過3.00的學生可以申請獎學金。

英文範例

【★可替換其他問題】

寫信詢問留學課程

Dear Mr. Wang,   ● 對象

Thank you so much for providing information about business schools in the U.S.A. I've read the files for all the top-ranking business schools, and I'm very interested in applying to the one-year full-time MBA programs in University of Southern California.

Here are still some questions I'd like to consult you about the above program:

★ 1. How many students typically participate in this program?
   2. How many international students study at this school?   ● 內容
   3. What are the language requirements for international students?   ● 內容
   4. Are language requirements fulfilled while abroad? Or do they provide immersion program on-site?   ● 內容
   5. What's the GPA requirement for admission?
   6. Is there scholarship or financial aids available for international students?   ● 內容
                                                                                                        ● 內容
                                                                                                        ● 內容

I would much appreciate it if you could to the above questions a.s.a.p.

Sincerely,
Jordan Liao

段落大意

寫信目的	開場先感謝對方協助申請留學，註明學校等基本資訊。
詢問細節	詢問留學資訊。
敬請回覆	要求對方收到訊息後回覆。
信尾	客套語 ＋ 署名。

中文翻譯

王先生您好：

十分感謝您提供美國商學院相關資料。我已經閱讀過所有美國頂尖商學院的資料，我對於申請南加大為期一年的MBA課程很感興趣。

以下是我針對此課程的疑問，想諮詢您的意見：
1. 通常攻讀該學位的學生有多少人？
2. 該校有多少國際學生？
3. 國際學生的入學英語標準為何？
4. 在就讀前就得先在海外達到英語標準嗎？還是校方有提供國際學生到校後，就讀語言銜接課程？
5. 申請入學的平均學業成績為何？
6. 有提供國際學生獎學金或財務上的協助嗎？

若您能盡速回答以上疑惑，將不勝感激。

Jordan Liao 敬上

換個對象寫寫看

費用部分

- I'd like to know how much money I have to prepare for this one year program, including tuition, books, housing, meals, special excursions, and a round-way airfare. Since costs are my primary concern, I'm wondering if there are scholarships, financial aid available for international students.

  我想要知道這一年的費用大致上我要準備多少。包含學費，書籍費用，住宿，餐飲，校外教學，以及一張來回機票。因為費用是我主要選校考量的指標，所以我想詢問該校是否提供國際學生獎助學金？

住宿家庭或住宿安排

- I'd like to know more about accommodation arrangements. The questions are as follows.
  1. How many types of housing arrangements are there to choose from?
  2. How far is the housing from the university?
  3. Are meals included?
  4. Can the program accommodate students with special dietary needs (e.g. food allergies)?

  我想知道更多有關住宿的安排。以下是我的疑問：
  1. 有多少種類的住宿可以選擇？
  2. 住宿地點距離學校約多近？
  3. 有提供伙食嗎？
  4. 是否可以照顧有特殊飲食需求的學生（食物過敏）？

其他詢問留學顧問有關課程的問句

1. Does the school offer postgraduate courses within my major?
   這所學校是否有提供和我目前主修科目相關的碩士課程？
2. I'd like to know how long it takes to graduate. And I'd like to know the classes are offered regularly.
   我想知道修業時間（就讀到畢業會花多久時間）。我也想要知道所有科目是否按時開課。

句型解說在這裡

句型1

have / has + p.p.

使用時機：
1. 過去開始的動作（但沒有明確的時間），到現在前已經完成。有時會有關鍵字already, just, yet.
   - The professor has already read our reports, but he hasn't graded them yet.
     教授已經看過我們的報告，但還沒打成績。
2. 過去開始的動作（但沒有明確的時間），到現在仍在持續中。關鍵字for, since
   - He has had a cold for more than a week. He hasn't come to school since last Tuesday.
     他已經感冒超過一個星期了。他從上週二到現在都沒來上學。
3. 從過去到現在累積的經驗或次數。關鍵字once, twice, many times, before, ever.
   - A: Have you ever been to Tokyo Disneyland? 你去過東京迪士尼樂園嗎？
     B: Yes, I've been there twice. 是的，我去過兩次。

句型2

adj.-現在分詞／過去分詞

觀念：
1. 形容詞-現在分詞(V-ing)：被形容的名詞當主詞時，動詞用主動語態
   例：a top-ranking （排名頂尖的）school → a school which ranks top
   　　wide-ranging （廣泛的）discussions → discussions which range wide
   　　loose-fitting （鬆身的）clothes → clothes which fit loose
2. 形容詞-過去分詞(p.p.)：被形容的名詞當主詞時，動詞用被動語態
   例：a high-priced （高價的） designer handbag → a designer handbag which is priced high
   　　a low-paid （低薪的）job → a job which is paid low

練習時間試試看

對於留學的課程有不明白，寫信詢問

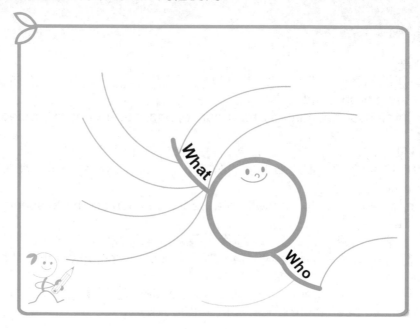

 Who are you writing to?

 What do you want to know about?

練習範例分享

Dear Ms. Brown,　————————————→ 對象

I'm very interested in off-site online MBA programs
offered in _____University.

Here are still some questions I'd like to consult you
about the above program:

1. Are ALL courses for this degrees offered online?　————→ 內容
2. How are the online courses delivered?　————→ 內容
3. How do students interact with the instructor and each
   other?　————————————→ 內容
4. What are the admissions deadlines?　————→ 內容
5. How many credits are required for a degree?　————→ 內容
6. Are course grades based on test scores, essays, or
   both?　————————————→ 內容

I would much appreciate if you could to the above
questions a.s.a.p.

Sincerely,
Jenny Huang

Brown 小姐您好：
我對於____大學的線上MBA課程很感興趣。

以下是我針對此課程的疑問，想諮詢您的意見：
1. 這個學程的所有課程都是可以線上學習的嗎？
2. 線上課程的上課方式為何？
3. 學生和講師如何互動？
4. 申請截止時間為何？
5. 需要修幾個學分才能取得學位？
6. 學科評分的標準是考試或是報告，或兩者皆為評分標準？

若您能盡速回答以上疑惑，將不勝感激。

Jenny Huang　敬上

Unit 6

留學

情境一
申請學校

情境二
詢問宿舍／住宿
家庭

情境三
詢問課程

情境一 申請學校

心智圖解說

寫作技巧錦囊

Who are you writing to? 寫給誰？
→ Ms. Kelly Smith

What program do you apply to? 申請什麼課程？
→ Master of Environmental Management

When will you commence your study? 什麼時候開始？
→ commence study in semester 1, 2014

most commonly included **categories** in the motivation letter: 類別
→ Objective, Education, Experience, Employment, Certifications

單字片語搶先看

1. master *n.[C]* 碩士 *(=postgraduate)*
   ☞ I was just admitted to the master program in the graduate school.
   我才剛申請錄取這所研究所的碩士課程。

2. management *n.[U]* 管理
   ☞ This position requires at least 2 years of work experience in business management.
   這份職務需要兩年以上商管經驗。
   詞類變化：manage *vi. vt.* 管理

3. procedure *n.[C]* 程序
   ☞ A typical admissions procedure takes about 1 month.
   一般入學申請程序約需一個月的時間。

4. bachelor *adj.* 學士的 *(=undergraduate)*
   ☞ Please enclose a certified copy of your bachelor degree to your application.
   請在申請表上附上一份驗證過的學士學位副本。

5. internship *n.[C]* 實習工作
   ☞ Terry did well in his internship and thus got a full-time position in the company.
   Terry在實習期間表現傑出，因此得到了正職的職位。
   相關字詞：intern *n.[C]* 實習生

6. specialty *n.[C]* 專長
   ☞ This photographer's specialty is night photography.
   這位攝影師的專長是夜間攝影。

7. theoretical *adj.* 理論上的
   ☞ She has theoretical knowledge of teaching, but no practical experience.
   她有教學的理論知識，但沒有實務經驗。
   詞類變化：theory *n.[C]* 理論

8. practical *adj.* 實務上的
   ☞ She cultivates practical experience in fashion design by running her own workshop.
   她藉著開個人工作室，不斷累積時裝設計的實務經驗。
   詞類變化：practice *n.[C]* 實務

英文範例

【★可加入其他對於工作經歷等敘述】

申請學校

Dear Sir or Madam,

對象

I am writing to you to express my interest in applying for Master of Environmental Management in the University of Queensland, scheduled to start in February 2014. I appreciate this opportunity and I would like to provide further information in support of my admission procedure.

內容

何時

I am about to graduate with a bachelor's degree in Environmental Science from National Taiwan University in June 2013. I have maintained very good marks in all important and relevant subjects. I also had an internship for an environmental consultancy during summer vacation. Throughout my college years, I have realized that environmental management is the specialty where I want to focus on.

★ As my aim is to work in an environmental consultancy, I believe the high reputation of your University in the environmental sciences, and the courses in this program would provide me with the necessary theoretical knowledge and practical skills I will need to succeed as a urban environmental management advisor in the future.

類別

I am aware of the highly competitive demands of this master's program, but I am confident that I have the ability, ambition and motivation to exceed the requirements and I will do my best to excel within the program. I would like to mention that I also have the support from two recognized lecturers of National Taiwan University. I am sure that my academic performance, deep concern in environmental management and willingness to make a progress make me a very good candidate and will add diversity to this master's degree program.

類別

類別

Thank you very much for considering my request. I look forward to your positive response.

Yours faithfully,
Laura Chu

段落大意

寫信目的	開場直接說明你要申請的校系和入學時間。
學經歷背景介紹	分段簡述申請該校系的原因、相關學歷和工作經歷。
敬請回覆	要求對方回覆確認。
信尾	客套語 + 署名。

中文翻譯

先生、小姐您好，

我寫信來申請2014年二月入學的昆士蘭大學環境管理碩士課程。我感謝有這個機會可以向您提供更多入學申請相關資訊。

我即將在2013年六月從台大環境科學系畢業。我在所有重要相關科目都維持很好的成績。我也在暑假期間在環境顧問公司擔任實習生。在我大學求學期間，我發現我想要更專注發展環境管理這個專業領域，我希望未來能在環境管理諮詢這個領域工作，因此我相信貴校在環境科學領域的卓越聲譽及相關課程，能幫助我取得理論和實務上的所必須具備的專業技能，讓我日後可以成為一位都市環境管理專業顧問。

我知道該課程入學要求很高，但我有信心我有能力、抱負和動機通過這些入學條件，入學後我會盡全力有良好的表現。我也想特別提出我得到兩位台大高知名度講師的支持。相信我的學業表現、對環境管理的高度關注、以及努力追求進步的決心讓我成為很好的申請者，也能為碩士班注入一股新血。

非常謝謝您考慮我的申請。期待能收到正面的回應。

Laura 朱 敬上

換個對象寫寫看

相關實習或社團經驗

◦ I was selected to do an internship for an environmental consultancy in Taipei City for two months during summer vacation in 2011. This experience allowed me with the possibility to gain a valuable and practical knowledge in the consultancy and environmental advice, areas which I would like to develop my future career in.

我在2011年暑期在台北市一家環境顧問公司擔任實習生，工作了兩個月，這個經驗讓我有機會學習和環境管理有關、寶貴的實務經驗，這也是我未來想投入的職場。

相關工作經驗

◦ Soon after graduating, I started working as a project assistant in a prestigious environmental consulting company for six months. I have participated in more than five international projects and have learned a lot from the colleagues I work with and gained a lot of experience in team working and communication skills.

畢業後不久我就開始在頗負盛名的環境管理顧問公司工作，擔任專案助理六個月。這期間我參與了五個國際專案，從同事身上學到了很多，也得到很多團隊工作和溝通技巧上的經驗。

其他申請學校自傳的萬用語

1. I'd like to pursue further education in this field to gain deeper theoretical and practical knowledge and achieve the career goals I have set for myself, taking a step forward for my professional development in this particular field.
   我想要進一步進修該領域，以取得更深入的學理和實務知識，並達成我為自己設定的職涯目標，進一步追求在這個領域的專業發展。
2. My academic performance has been always on top of class. I have been an active member of the IT League Academy in Taiwan where I have been involved in the development of several software projects
   我的學業成績一直在班上名利前茅。我也在台灣IT學術聯盟表現活躍，在這個聯盟裡，我參與設計了幾款軟體開發專案。
3. I have enclosed all materials required for acceptance into the master's program. Thank you very much for your consideration of my application.
   我已經附上所有碩士課程申請所需文件。謝謝您過目我的申請。

句型解說在這裡

句型1

> be about to V　　即將

○ The train is about to leave in a minute. Hurry up.
　火車再過一分鐘就要開了。快一點。

延伸觀念

一般未來式的用法
1. will + VR　表示未來的時間狀態語（tomorrow, next）
○ I will help you when I finish my homework.
　等我寫完功課就會幫你。
2. be going to V　多用於口語中，表示已計畫好的未來、將要發生的事
○ We are going to see a movie tonight.
　我們計畫好今晚要去看電影。
3. come / go / leave / start出發 / begin / arrive / depart / stay等動詞用「現在進行式」表示計畫將要做的動作
○ They are leaving for New York tonight.
　今晚他們將要動身前往紐約。
　= They are going to leave…
　= They are about to leave…

句型2

> my aim / goal / dream is + to V　　我的目標／夢想是去做……

○ My aim is to work in the fashion industry.
　我的目標是在時尚界工作。

句型觀念

to V 不定詞片語就是主詞(my aim / goal / dream) 在be動詞後方的補語
○ My dream is to travel around the world.
　我的夢想是環遊世界。
○ His goal is to be the best golfer in the world.
　他的目標是成為世界第一的高爾夫球選手。

練習時間試試看

申請學校

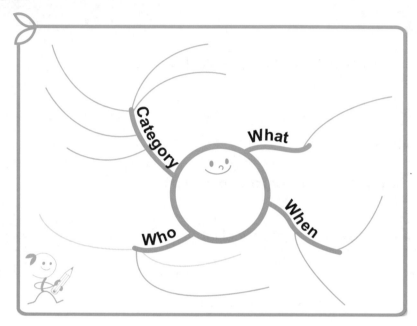

 Who are you writing to?

 What program do you apply to?

 When will you commence your study?

 Most commonly included categories in the motivation letter:

練習範例分享

Dear Sir or Madam,　　　　　　　　　　　對象

I hereby apply for entrance to the Master Program on Design and Construction Project Management at the Chalmers University of Technology for the 2013 autumn term. I am very interested in this degree and I believe my strong academic background in Engineering combined with my work experience will fulfill your requirements.　　申請什麼課程 何時

I graduated from National Central University with a bachelor degree in Civil Engineering. On my 4 years Civil Engineering degree I got specialized in concrete structures and I also formed good knowledge in Planning and Transportation.　　類別

After graduation, I have been working as a site manager for a Project Management firm where I am improving my skills in construction management and site coordination. After 4 years of professional experience on the construction business, I have decided this is the field that I want to be specialized in. And your Master Program will contribute to the evolution of my career as it suits perfectly as an upgrade of the current position I hold and will allow me to develop my skills on Project Management.　　類別

I have enclosed all materials required for acceptance into the master's program. Thank you very much for your consideration of my application.

Yours sincerely,
William Hsu

先生、小姐您好，

我寫信來申請就讀Chalmers科技大學工程設計營建專案管理碩士課程2013年秋季班。我對這個課程很有興趣，我相信以我在工程的學術背景和相關工作經驗，可以滿足入學的條件。
我是中央大學土木工程系畢業。在這四年求學期間，我對於混泥土結構有專業的知識，也對營造計畫和交通有很好的概念。

在畢業後，我在一家營建管理公司工作，擔任工地監工。這份工作讓我精進工程管理和工地聯繫溝通技巧，在營建業工作四年之後，我認為這是我未來想要專精的領域。而你們的碩士課程能提升我未來職場競爭力，因為它能幫助我工作晉升並加強我在專案管理所需的能力。

我已經附上所有碩士課程申請所需文件。謝謝您考慮我的申請。

William 徐　敬上

情境二 詢問宿舍／住宿家庭

心智圖解說

寫作技巧錦囊

Who are you writing to?　寫給誰？
→ Mr. Dennis Wills

What do you request?　要求什麼？
→ arranging home stay

Types of accommodation offered　住宿種類
→ host families

Questions　問題
→ Fees, regulations / rules, location / transportation, host family information, special request

單字片語搶先看

1. **concerning** *prep.* 關於…… *(=regarding, about)*
   - I have several questions regarding the terms of the lease.
   我對於這個房屋租賃契約的條款有一些疑問。

2. **placement** *n.[U]* 安置，安排 *(= arrangement)*
   - The Student Affairs Office charges $20 for dormitory placement for freshmen.
   學生事務處針對大一新生安排宿舍會收取20美金的安置費用。

3. **institution** *n.[C]* 機構
   - He just enrolled in an English course at this language institution.
   他剛在這家語言學習機構報名了一門英語課程。

4. **sign up for** 註冊；報名 *(= enroll in, register)*
   - He's going to sign up for a swimming class.
   他將要報名一堂游泳課。

5. **lease** *n.[C]* 房屋租賃契約
   - Tenants need to make sure they understand and agree to all the terms in the lease.
   房客必須確認瞭解並同意所有房屋租賃契約上的條款。

6. **security deposit** 押金
   - How will the landlord return the full amount of security deposit?
   房東在什麼條件下會全額退還押金？

7. **rent** *n.[C,U]* 租金；租費
   - Most tenants are asked to pay the rent at the beginning of every month.
   大部分房客都被要求要在每個月月初繳付房租。

英文範例

【★可代換其他問題】

詢問宿舍／住宿家庭

Dear Ms. Smith, ————————————— 對象

I am writing to inquire about the "English and homestay
program" provided by HES Language School. I am
a college student from Taiwan. I will be coming to ————— 為什麼
New Zealand for three months from June 16th to
September 15th, 2013. I would like to stay with a host
family during my stay, but I have some questions about —— 種類
accommodation arrangement and would like to consult
you in advance.

★ My questions are mainly concerning fees. Do I need
to pay homestay placement fee to your institution? Or
do you book accommodation for students who sign up
for English courses for free? Besides, do I need to pay
for airport pick-up? How much do I pay the homestay
family every month? Will you help me sign the lease?
Do I need to pay security deposit along with my first
month's rent at the same time when I arrive? If yes,
how much is the deposit? Will I get the full deposit back
when I leave? ————————————————— 問題

I would very much appreciate it if you can respond to
the above questions at your early convenience.

Yours Sincerely,
Jessica Ma

段落大意

寫信目的　開場先說明自己入住的時間。

細節　詢問住宿家庭的細節。

敬請回覆　要求對方收到訊息後回覆確認。

信尾　客套語 + 署名。

中文翻譯

Smith小姐您好：

我寫信詢問有關HES語言學校所提供的「語言課程+寄宿家庭方案」。我是台灣來的大學生。我從2013年6月16日起會到紐西蘭待三個月到9月15日。我想住在寄宿家庭，但我關於住宿的安排有一些疑問，想要事先跟您諮詢。

我主要的疑問都和費用有關。我要付住宿安排費給你們機構嗎？還是你們對於報名語言課程的學生提供免費住宿安排的服務？此外，我若要求機場接送會需要額外付費嗎？我每個月要付給住宿家庭多少費用？你們會協助我和住宿家庭簽約嗎？我是否要在抵達時先繳第一個月的房租和押金？如果是的話，押金多少錢？等我要離開前，押金會全額退給我嗎？

若您能盡速撥冗回覆以上問題，我將萬分感激。

Jessica 馬　敬上

換個對象寫寫看

關於大學宿舍

I'd like to stay at the on-campus dormitory. But prior to my application, I'd like to consult you about the following questions. First of all, when can I check in and check out? Since I have some research to continue during summer, can I stay in the dorm during the summer vacation? Besides, I have some concerns about getting alone with roommates. Can I request to stay with local students during the application? Can I change my room if I don't get along with my roommate?

我對於你們的校內宿舍感興趣。但在我申請前,我想詢問以下問題。首先,入宿和退宿的日期是什麼時候?因為我在暑假期間還要繼續進行研究,暑期可以住宿嗎?此外,我對於和室友相處有些顧慮。我可以在申請時選擇要和當地學生同住一個寢室嗎?若我和室友處不來,可以換寢室嗎?

關於住宿人員分配、設備和服務相關問題

I have some questions regarding student shared apartments. Do males and females have separate or mixed accommodations? How many people share an apartment? Are there facilities for washing and drying clothes? What appliances are permitted in student rooms? What kinds of housekeeping services are provided?

我對於學生分租公寓有以下的疑問。男生和女生分開住或混合住宿?多少人一起分租一個公寓?公寓裡有洗衣和乾衣的設備嗎?學生房間內可以攜帶哪些類型的家電用品?是否有提供打掃的服務?

其他常見的住宿相關疑問

1. Is there a meal plan that comes with my housing options?
   住宿方案有沒有結合訂餐相關的配套?
2. Where can I stay if I arrive before or depart after the housing contract begins or ends?
   若我在住宿合約入宿日期前抵達,或合約結束後要多留幾天,我可以住在哪裡?

句型解說在這裡

句型1

along with + n. 連同

☞ Meals are included in the rent, along with cable and the Internet.
伙食費包含在房租裡，連同有線電視和網路費。

延伸觀念

A along with / together with / as well as B：「A連同B」，主詞是A，
決定動詞單複數

☞ The security guard along with two customers was held hostage.
警衛連同兩位顧客一起被挾持作人質。
（語法上真正的主詞是the security guard，單數名詞，接單數動詞 was）

(both) A and B：「A和B」，主詞是A+B，接複數動詞

☞ The security guard and two customers were held hostage.
警衛和兩位顧客一起被挾持作人質。
（主詞是the security guard and the two customers，複數名詞，接複數動詞were）

句型2

when + 現在簡單式 代表未來式

觀念：從屬連接詞（when, if, after, before, as long as…）引導的子句要用現在簡單式代替未來式

☞ Will I get my full deposit when I leave?
當我離開的時候，我能拿回全額押金嗎？
→主要子句 Will I get my full deposit 保留未來式
→由 when 引導的附屬子句 when I leave 用現在簡單式代替未來式

☞ If it rains tomorrow, let's cancel the outdoor barbecue. 如果明天下雨，我們就取消戶外烤肉。
→主要子句 let's cancel the outdoor barbecue 保留祈使句
→由 If 引導的附屬子句 If it rains tomorrow 用現在簡單式代替未來式

練習時間試試看

收到住宿家庭資料，進一步詢問相關訊息

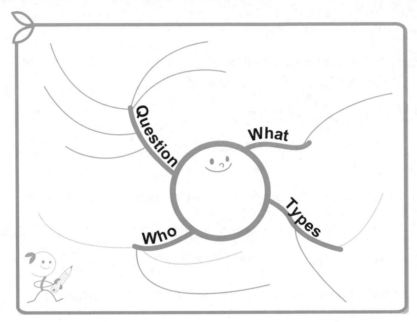

 Who are you writing to?

 What do you request?

 Questions

練習範例分享

Dear Mr. Josh Whitman,

Thank you for processing my homestay request form promptly.
I have received your email yesterday regarding the homstay
arrangement. I have read the background information about
my host family, Mr. and Mrs. Benjamin Brownings. But I'd
like to know more about them and homestay location.

誰
為什麼

Regarding my host family, do they accommodate other
international students the same time during my stay? In
addition, I have mentioned in my request form that I'm
allergic to seafood and I don't eat beef. Are they OK with my
dietary requirements?

問題

I'm also concerned about the location of the homestay. Is it
near any public transportation? How long does it take to go
to school from the homestay? Is it convenient to get around
the city?

問題

I would very much appreciate it if you can respond to the
above questions at your early convenience.

問題

Yours sincerely,
Jack Peterson

Josh Whitman先生您好：

謝謝您盡速處理了我的住宿家庭需求表。我昨天收到了您的電子郵件，得知您已經
為我安排好住宿家庭。我已經讀過我的住宿家庭主人Benjamin Brownings夫婦的背
景資料。但我想詢問更多有關他們和住宿地點的細節。

關於我的住宿家庭，在我投宿期間，他們是否也接待其他的國際學生呢？此外，我
在住宿需求表上有註明，我對海鮮過敏且不吃牛肉。他們可以接受我在飲食上面的
需求嗎？

我同時也關心我住宿的地點。它是否鄰近公共交通運輸系統？從住宿家庭到學校大
約要花多久時間？要到市區走動是否方便？

若您能盡速撥冗回覆以上問題，我將萬分感激。

Jack Peterson　敬上

情境三　詢問課程

心智圖解說

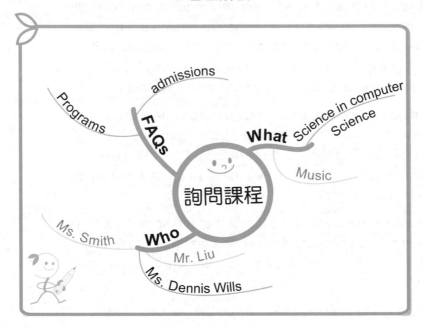

寫作技巧錦囊

Who are writing to?　寫給誰？
→ Ms Emma Core

What course / program are you interested in?
對什麼課程有興趣？
→ Master of Science in Computer Science

FAQs (Frequently asked Questions)　常見問題
→ Admissions, Programs / Units / Courses

單字片語搶先看

1. **faculty** *n.[C]* (大學)系、科、學院
   - I've just consulted a faculty member regarding the bridging course.
   我剛和教員諮詢了銜接課程的事宜。

2. **undergraduate** *adj. n.[C]* 學士；大學部
   - She had an undergraduate degree in psychology.
   她有心理學學士學位。

3. **postgraduate** *adj. n.[C]* 碩士；研究所*(Br. E)* 博士後 *(Am. E)*
   - She is currently studying a postgraduate degree in Musical Therapy at University of Melbourne.
   她目前正在墨爾本大學攻讀音樂治療的碩士學位。

4. **coursework** *n.[U]* 授課課程
   - Most students in Taiwan go to Australia for postgraduate coursework programs.
   大部分台灣赴澳洲深造者選擇攻讀授課型的碩士課程。

5. **curriculum** *n.[C]* 課程
   - IT is now on the curriculum in most schools.
   資訊科技現在已經是大多數學校的課程之一。

6. **unit** *n.[C]* 學分
   - How many units should I gain to earn a master's degree?
   我要修多少學分才能拿到碩士學位？

7. **elective** *adj.* 選修的
   - Elective units are courses that students can choose to take, but they do not have to take it in order to graduate.
   選修學分指的是學生可以選修的學分，但並非取得學位必修的學分。

8. **remotely** *adv.* 遠距的
   - Distance Learning education are gaining its popularity because courses are taught remotely.
   遠距教學越來越受歡迎，因為遠距離傳授課程。

英文範例

【★可代換其他疑問】

詢問課程

Dear Ms Emma Core,

　　　　　　　　　　　　　　　　　　　　● 對象

I'm very interested in the Master of Science in Computer Science provided by Faculty of Science, University of Sydney. I'm currently completing my

　　　　　　　　　　　　　　　　　　　　● 內容

undergraduate degree in Engineering at University of Melbourne, and I'd like to apply to the above postgraduate coursework program upon my graduation. But there are some questions I have regarding the admissions, and curriculum.

★ Regarding admissions, what would be the minimum GPA required to apply to the MS CS? Do you have to be a Computer Science undergraduate major to apply? As for the courses, what is the minimum number of units I can take per quarter? What courses can I count as Electives on my program sheet? Last but not least, what classes are offered remotely?

　　　　　　　　　　　　　　　　　　　　● 常見問題

Thank you again for your time with my request and I would much appreciate if you could respond to the above questions a.s.a.p.

Sincerely,

Oscar Wang

段落大意

寫信目的	開場先說明有興趣的科系。
細節	索取課程細節。
敬請回覆	要求對方收到訊息後回覆確認。
信尾	客套語 + 署名。

中文翻譯

Emma Core女士您好：

我對於雪梨大學的理科碩士學位-電腦科學碩士課程很感興趣。我目前還在墨爾本大學就讀工程學學士學位，我想在畢業時，申請了上述碩士課程。但對於入學條件和課程我有以下疑問。

首先跟入學條件有關，要申請電腦科學碩士課程的平均成績最低要達幾分？是否必須大學主修電腦科學系才能申請該碩士課程？至於課程本身，我每一季最少要修多少學分？在我課程選單上哪些課程算是選修學分？最後，有哪些課程可以透過遠距教學授課？

若您能盡速回答以上疑惑，將不勝感激。

Oscar 王　敬上

換個對象寫寫看

研究類型的課程疑問

☞ What research degrees are available at this faculty? How can I search for a research supervisor and project? As I notice that there is flexibility in whether my degree is undertaken on a full or part-time basis, or whether the studies are campus-based or off campus. But can you give me a rough idea of how much time it usually takes if I study full-time on campus?

在該學院有哪些研究型的課程，以及我該如何找到指導教授和研究主題？我注意到研究型學士後課程授課方式很彈性，可以選擇全天或半天課程，也可以在校或不需到校上課。但您是否可以給我一個大概的概念，通常，唸全日到校的密集課程說修業時間大約多長？

財務支持

☞ What will my fees be and is there any financial support available to international students? Where can I get information about applying for scholarships? Besides, can the faculty member or the Student Affairs Officer assist me in finding a TA(teaching assistant) or RA(research assistant) position?

我的費用預估要多少，是否提供國際學生財務協助？哪裡可以取得申請獎學金相關的訊息？此外，教員或是學生事務處人員可否協助我找到助教或研究助理的職務？

其他詢問留學顧問有關課程的問句

1. Which specialization should I consider if I want to study Master by Research program in the faculty?
   如果我要唸該學院研究型的課程，哪一種領域我可以考慮？

句型解說在這裡

句型1

am / is / are + V-ing　　現在進行式

使用時機：
1. 現在說話這一刻正在發生的事。關鍵字now, at the moment
☞ He is talking on the phone at the moment. Do you want to wait on the line?
他現在還在講電話。你要在線上等候嗎？
2. 雖然非現在這一刻正在動作，但是這段期間以來持續中的事件。關鍵字currently, this year
☞ He is currently taking a guitar lesson at the music school.
他最近在音樂學校學彈吉他。
3. 來去動詞（go / come / leave / arrive / stay…）以現在進行式代替未來式.
☞ We're going to a movie tonight. Are you coming with us?
我們今晚要去看電影，你要不要一起來？

Last but not least,......　　最後一點，……

舉列例子或論點的轉承詞：放在句子前，以逗點隔開
1. 舉出第一個論點「首先」：to begin with, to start with, first, firstly
2. 舉出第2個或接續的論點「第二，其次，接著，此外」：second, secondly, then, besides, in addition, also, moreover, furthermore, what's more
3. 舉出最後一個論點「最後」：Finally, Last (but not least)

練習時間試試看

對於遊學的課程有不明白，寫信詢問

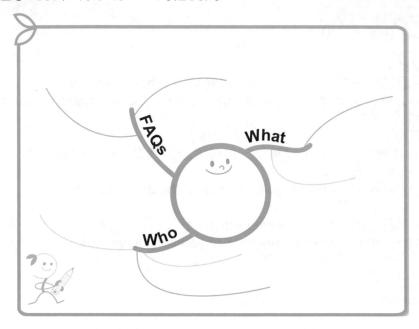

 Who are you writing to?

 What course / program are you interested in?

 FAQs (Frequently asked Questions)

練習範例分享

Dear Ms. Kelly Lively,
　　　　　　　　　　　　　　　　　　　　• 對象

I'm very interested in the short-term College study
abroad tour in London provided by EF International.
　　　　　　　　　　　　　　　　　　　　• 內容
I've read your brochure and online introduction to
the program, but there are some questions I have
regarding the program details and schedule.

I'm wondering if we can join the activities with local
students during the tour. I'm also curious about how
much time will be on academic classroom learning and
how much will be spent touring? What is an optional
excursion? How much free time does my group have to
organize a private tour?
　　　　　　　　　　　　　　　　　　　　• 常見問題
Thank you again for your time with my request and I
would much appreciate it if you could respond to the
above questions a.s.a.p.

Sincerely
Bruce Wayne

Kelly Lively女士您好：

我對於EF國際教育機構舉辦的倫敦短期大學遊學團很感興趣。我已經看過你們的手冊和網路的介紹，但還是有關於課程相關的問題想要詢問您。

我想知道在遊學期間，我們是否可以跟當地學生一起參與活動。我也很想知道會花多少時間在教室上課，以及多少時間旅遊。自選行程又是什麼？我的團有多少時間可以安排私人行程？

若您能盡速回答以上疑惑，將不勝感激。

Bruce Wayne　敬上

Unit 7

求職

 情境一
寫履歷

 情境二
更改面試時間

 情境三
詢問面試結果

情境一　寫履歷

心智圖解說

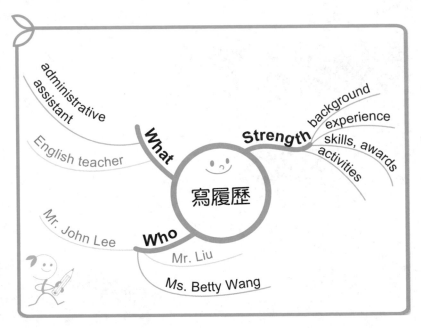

寫作技巧錦囊

Who are you writing to?　對象
→ Ms. Betty Wang

What position you are applying for?　應徵職位
→ administrative assistant

Strength　優勢
→ background, work experience, skills, awards, extra-curricular activities

單字片語搶先看

1. enthusiasm *n.[C,U]* 熱心；熱情；熱忱
   ☞ This new employee works with enthusiasm.
   這位新進員工以無比的熱忱工作。
   詞類變化：enthusiastic *adj.* 熱情的

2. administrative assistant 行政助理
   ☞ Many college graduates apply for the position of administrative assistant.
   很多大學畢業生應徵這個行政助理的職缺。

3. resume *n.[C]* 履歷
   ☞ Cassie tailor-made her resume for the position of project manager.
   Cassie為應徵專案經理的工作，量身訂做寫履歷。

4. CV (Curriculum Vitae) 履歷
   ☞ You can send your CV with a cover letter or email asking if they have any vacancies in your trade.
   你可以用介紹信或電子郵件附上你的履歷，詢問他們是否有相關的工作職缺。

5. certificate *n.[C]* 證照
   ☞ Please enclose a degree certificate to your application form.
   請在你申請書上附上學位證書。

6. computer-literate *adj.* 熟悉電腦操作的
   ☞ Nowadays almost everyone should be computer-literate to deal with office work.
   現在幾乎人人都要熟悉電腦操作，才能處理辦公室事務。

7. strength *n.[C]* 長處；優點
   ☞ State your strengths in your resume, so the employer will consider your application.
   要在履歷表上說明你的長處，這樣雇主才會考慮你的申請。

英文範例

【★可加入其他對於自身優勢的敘述】

寫履歷

Dear Ms. Wang, — 對象

I am writing with enthusiasm to apply for the position of
administrative assistant listed on 104 Job Bank. I hope — 內容
you can see from the enclosed resume and CV that I'm
perfect and well-qualified for this job.

★ I majored in English in Fu Jen Catholic University. I
have also attached my language proficiency certificates
to show that I have good command of English. I also
have 3 years of related administrative experience in my
previous job, and I'm computer-literate and skilled at
routine office work. — 優勢

I would be very grateful for your consideration, and I am
available to come for an interview at your convenience
to fully explain my strength and qualifications. You can
reach me at 22145212.

I'm looking forward to hearing from you soon.

Sincerely Yours,
Emma Liao

段落大意

寫信目的　開場直接說明你要申請的職務以及自己最相關的專長。

學經歷背景介紹細節　分段簡述相關學歷和工作經歷、或熱情展現對於新工作和該公司的抱負。

感謝與懇請回覆　要求對方回覆確認約面試時間。

信尾　客套語 ＋ 署名。

中文翻譯

王小姐您好，

我很熱忱寫信要應徵貴公司在104人力銀行上行政助理一職。希望您能從我附件的履歷表和個人學經歷列表中，看到我能完全勝任這項職務，而且是這份工作的最佳人選。

我在輔仁大學主修英語，並附上語言認證資料展以證明我有絕佳英文能力。我在前一份工作也累積有三年行政相關經驗，我對於電腦使用很上手，也熟悉日常辦公事務。

若蒙考慮，我將不勝感激，我也能配合您方便的時間前來面試，以充分說明我的長處和相關經歷。請打電話和我聯繫，電話號碼是22145212。

期待您的回音。

Emma 廖　敬上

換個對象寫寫看

社會新鮮人：強調學業上傑出表現或社團經驗

- During my studies at the college, insurance and financial planning are my fields of special interest and expertise. I completed related courses with high grades. And I have obtained various financial certificates such as Proficiency Test for Financial Planning Personnel. I also participated actively in extra-curricular activities at the university and have gained experiences at organizing events or teamwork and leadership.

 在我讀大學期間，保險和財務規劃是我的興趣與專長。我以高分修得相關學分，我取得多種財務金融相關證照，例如理財規劃人員專業證照。我也熱衷投入課外社團活動，累積了企劃活動、團體合作以及領導能力。

個人特質優勢分析

- I see myself as results-oriented, high-energy with hands-on professional experiences in this specific field. Major strengths include strong leadership, excellent communication skills, competent, strong team player, attention to details, dutiful respect for compliance in all regulated environments, as well as supervisory skills including hiring, termination, scheduling, training, payroll, and other administrative tasks. I possess thorough knowledge of this industry, and a clear vision to accomplish the company goals. I'm also computer and Internet literate.

 我認為我自己是以結果為導向、活力充沛，在此相關領域累積了很多實務經驗。我的主要優勢包含很強的領導能力、絕佳的人際溝通技巧、有能力、也和團體合作融洽、注意細節、克竟職責、尊崇公司的制度與規定，也具備監督管理能力，對於人員聘僱與解職、進度規劃、人員訓練、薪資管理等行政工作也有涉獵。對於這個業界充分的了解，也有清晰的視野可以完成公司的目標並熟悉電腦和網路的操作。

其他自我推銷的萬用語

1. 懇請對方參考附件的履歷並給予面試機會：
   Please refer to my enclosed resume for more details. I hope you can consider my application.
   請詳閱附件的履歷以得到更多資訊。希望您能考慮我的申請。

句型解說在這裡

句型1

major in 主修	☞ Sandy majors in Electrical Engineering in college. Sandy在大學主修電子工程。

延伸觀念

minor in 副修	☞ She majors in Nursing and minors in Health Management. 她主修醫護，副修健康管理。
specialize in 專長於	☞ This doctor specializes in rehabilitation. 這位醫生的專長是復建。
be experienced in 在……方面很有經驗	☞ This senior employee is experienced in editing news clips. 這位資深員工在新聞編輯方面很有經驗。

句型2

have a good command of + 語言　　擅長……語言

☞ She was born and raised in Spain, so she has a good command of Spanish.
她在西班牙出生長大，所以她很懂西班牙文。

相關句型

be good at　　對……很擅長　　擅長……語言

☞ Mandy is good at translation and interpretation.
Mandy擅長翻譯與口譯。

be skilled at　　對……很擅長

☞ Aboriginal women are skilled in weaving and art craft.
原住民婦女擅長編織與製作手工藝品。

練習時間試試看

寫履歷

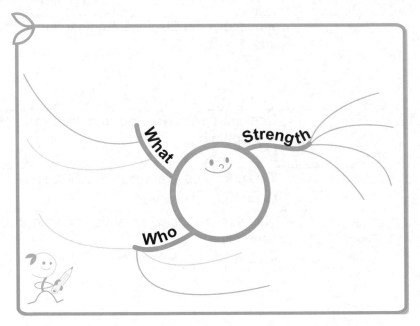

 Who are writing to?

 What position you are applying for?

 Strength

練習範例分享

Dear Ms. Wang,　　　　　　　　　　　　　對象

I am interested in the marketing assistant position
advertised in Times. I am currently employed as a　　內容
marketing personnel in XXX company. I have obtained
4 years of marketing experienced which are applicable
to your requirements for a marketing assistant.

My experience in my current job has afforded me the　　優勢
opportunity to become familiar with event organizing
and brand marketing. I also have extensive experience
in public relations. I believe my experience qualifies me
for consideration.

To further acquaint you with the specifics of my　　　優勢
background I am enclosing my resume. I hope you will
consider me for this position. I look forward to meeting
with you and discussing my qualifications in more
detail.

Sincerely,
Alice Hsu

王小姐您好，

我對於你們在時報上刊登應徵行銷助理的工作很感興趣。我目前就在……公司擔任
行銷人員。我累積了四年的行銷資歷，符合貴職務的條件要求。
我目前的工作讓我更瞭解活動規劃和品牌行銷，我對於公共關係也有很多經驗。我
相信這些經驗能讓我成為這份職務合適的人選。
為讓您更瞭解我相關的背景，附上我的履歷。希望您能考慮我的應徵。期待能和您
見面以進一步討論我的資歷。

Alice 徐 敬上

情境二　更改面試時間

心智圖解說

寫作技巧錦囊

Who are you writing to?　寫給誰？
→ Mr. Dennis Ho

What position you are applying for?　應徵的職位？
→ teaching assistant

Why do you need to change the date of interview?
更改面試日期的原因？
→ have an exam

單字片語搶先看

1. grateful *adj.* 感激的
   ☞ I'm very grateful to be offered this position.
   我很感激能得到這個職務。
   詞類變化：gratitude *n.[U]* 感激之情

2. opportunity *n.[C]* 機會 (= chance)
   ☞ This is an ideal opportunity to save money on a holiday to Hong Kong.
   這是一個存錢到香港度假的絕佳機會。

3. wonder *vi. vt.* 想知道
   ☞ I'm wondering if my application has been processed.
   我想知道我的申請案是否已經被處理了。

4. date *n.[C]* 日期
   ☞ I'm writing to request for change the interview date.
   我寫信來請求更改面試時間。

5. schedule *vt.* 排定行程
   ☞ The flight is scheduled to depart at 5:00 sharp.
   這班飛機預定五點整起飛。

6. available *adj.* 有空的
   ☞ Are you available for an interview this Friday afternoon at 2:00 pm?
   你本週五下午兩點是否有空可以來面試？

7. chance *n.[C]* 機會
   ☞ Can you give me another chance to be interviewed?
   能否再給我的機會與您面試？

英文範例

更改面試時間

Dear Mr. Ho, ————————————————————• 對象

Thank you very much for offering me an interview

for the position of teaching assistant. I am extremely

grateful for this opportunity, but I wonder if it would be ————• 內容

possible to change the interview date, ★ as my GEPT-

Intermediate level exam is already scheduled for

Saturday June 23rd. ————————————————————• 原因

I'm available in the afternoons from Monday to Friday.

I would be very pleased if you could change the date

and give me a chance to be interviewed.

Sincerely yours,

Karen Hsieh

段落大意

寫信目的　　開場先說明感謝對方給予面試機會，但要改時間。

細節　　改時間的原因和自己可以配合的時間。

敬請回覆　　要求對方收到訊息後回覆。

信尾　　客套語 + 署名。

中文翻譯

何先生您好：

很謝謝您願意讓我面試助教的職務，我很感激能有這個機會，但我想問是否可以改約其他面試日期，因為我的全民英檢中級考試恰巧也排在6月23日（週六）那一天。

我有空的時間是週一到週五下午的時段。若您能改約面試日期，讓我能來與您面談，我將非常感激。

Karen 謝　敬上

換個對象寫寫看

仍在工作中，無法請假面試

☞ Currently I'm still working, and thus I'm only available for the interview on Thursday afternoons. I would be very grateful if I can meet you then for the interview.

我現在仍在工作，因此我唯一有空的時間就是星期四下午。若能選擇該時段與您見面，我將非常感激。

當天有私人事務要處理

☞ Due to some urgent private matters that I need to deal with, I can only request to change the assigned interview date. I'm very interested in this position and sincerely hope I can still have a chance to be interviewed.

因為突發的私人事務要處理，我只能跟您請求更改面試日期。我對這個職務很有興趣，希望還是有機會可以跟您面試。

其他常見句型

1. I am extremely grateful for offering me an interview, but I wonder if it would be possible to change the interview date, as…

   我很感激您給我面試的機會，但我想知道有無可能可以更改面試日期，因為……。

2. I am very sorry that I'm not able to attend the interview on the scheduled date since I can't take a day off work.

   我很抱歉沒辦法依原定的時間來面試，因為當天我無法請假。

3. I would be very pleased if you could reschedule the date and give me an opportunity to be interviewed.

   若您能更改面試時間，給我個機會能與您面談，我將十分開心。

4. I'm very sorry for this short notice and inconvenience. I would be very grateful if you can still consider my application and offer me an opportunity for the interview.

   我很抱歉這麼臨時通知，造成您的不便。若您還是能考慮我的應徵，並給我機會面試，我將萬分感激。

句型解說在這裡

句型1

it is possible for 人 to V　　人做……是可能的

* It's possible for people to migrate to another planet.
  人類去外太空殖民是可能的。

延伸句型

it is + adj. + for 人 to V　　做……是……的

* It's easy to share your personal life on Facebook.
  在臉書上分享私人生活是很簡單的。
* It's convenient for people all over the world to meet online with the help of the Internet.
  拜網路所賜，世界各地的人要在網路上見面很方便。

句型2

if + 間接問句　　是否

間接問句：一個問句併入另一個句子中者，稱為間接問句
句型：主要子句 + 疑問詞（無疑問詞就用if / whether）+ S + V
* Who is he?（直接問句）
  → I don't know <u>who he is</u>.（間接問句）
* What do you want?（直接問句）
  → Tell me <u>what you want</u>.（間接問句）
* What does he want?（直接問句）
  → Do you know <u>what he wants</u>?（間接問句）
* Does he like you?（直接問句）
  → I'm wondering <u>if he likes you</u>.（間接問句）
  —— 沒疑問詞就用 if / whether 當疑問詞

練習時間試試看

更改面試時間

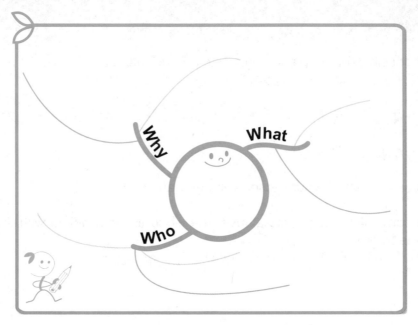

 Who are you writing to?

 What position you are applying for?

 Why do you need to change the date of interview?

練習範例分享

Dear Ms. Liao,　　　　　　　　　　　　　● 對象

I'm very grateful to be granted an interview for the position of editor of sports news. I've been reading　● 內容
your newspaper for years and have always dreamed of working as an editor in your company. However, I'm still working a full-time job and find it hard to take a day off for the scheduled interview. I was wondering if it　● 原因
would be possible to change the interview date to next Monday afternoon?

I would be very pleased if you could change the date and give me a chance to talk with you regarding the position.

Sincerely yours,
Betty Chang

廖小姐您好：

謝謝您願意讓我面試體育新聞編輯的職務。我很感激能有這個機會。我多年來一直是貴報紙忠實讀者，也一直夢想有一天能在你們公司工作。但由於我現在還有份全職的工作，原本預定要面試的那一天很難請假。我想問是否可以改約面試日期到下週一下午？

若您能改約面試日期，讓我能來與您面談，我將非常感激。

Betty 張　敬上

情境三　詢問面試結果

心智圖解說

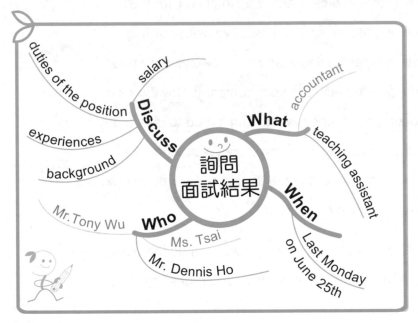

寫作技巧錦囊

 Who are you writing to?　寫給誰？
→ Mr. Dennis Ho

 What position you are applying for?　應徵職位？
→ teaching assistant

 When did you have an interview with the interviewer?　面試時間？
→ Last Monday on June 25th

 What did you **discuss** in the interview?　討論事項？
→ background and work experiences, duties of the position, salary requirements

單字片語搶先看

1. **personnel** *Plural n.* 員工 (=staff, employee)
   - All personnel are to receive security badges.
   所有職員都要佩帶識別證。

2. **well-established** *adj.* 發展健全的
   - She works in a well-established non-profit organization.
   她在一個發展健全的非營利組織工作。

3. **potential** *n.[C]* 潛力
   - A lot of ordinary people display their potentials in the talent show.
   很多素人在達人秀中展現他們的潛能。

4. **contribute** *vi. vt.* 捐獻；對……有所貢獻
   - I believe I can contribute a lot to this position and hope my application can be considered.
   我相信自己可以在這個職務一展長才，希望我的應徵可以被考慮。

5. **market** *vi. vt.* 購買；行銷
   - She has gained lots of practical experience in marketing and public relations.
   她在行銷和公關上累積很多實務經驗。

6. **line** *n.[C]* 系列
   - The designer brand has just launched its new lines of jeans.
   這個設計師品牌剛推出新的一系列牛仔褲。

7. **product** *n.[C]* 產品
   - The London factory assembles the finished producsts.
   倫敦的工廠負責組裝最後成品。

英文範例

【★可代換其他請求】

詢問面試結果

Dear Mr. Truman,   • 對象

Thank you so much for taking time out of your tight

schedule to interview me last Monday for the position

• 何時

of the marketing personnel. It was my pleasure to sit

• 內容

down and discuss my future possibilities with such

a well-established corporation as yours. I was very

impressed with the potential of your company and

sincerely hope I can contribute to marketing the new

lines of products.

• 討論事項

★ However, I haven't heard from you since the

interview. I'm wondering if the final decision has been

made regarding this position. I believe my experience

in marketing can be a great addition to this job and

hope my application can be reconsidered.

Thank you again and look forward to hearing from you

soon.

Sincerely,

Andrew Whitman

段落大意

寫信目的	開場先說明感謝對方撥冗與你面談，說明面試的職務與日期以提醒對方。
詢問	客氣提醒對方能回應是否已決定要錄取自己。
敬請回覆	請求對方收到訊息後儘快回覆確認。
信尾	客套語 + 署名。

中文翻譯

Truman先生您好：

很謝謝您上週在百忙之中，抽空和我面試有關行銷人員的職務。能坐下來與您討論貴公司那麼發展完善的公司的未來發展，真是我的榮幸。我也對貴公司的發展潛力留下深刻的印象，希望我能貢獻一己之力，有機會協助行銷最新系列的產品。

但從面試結束後到現在，我還沒接到您的回音。我想知道這份職務是否已經有定案了？相信以我在行銷的經驗，必定能在該職務上帶來很大的助益，希望您能再考慮一下我的應徵。

再次感謝您，希望能盡快得到您的消息。

Andrew Whitman　敬上

換個對象寫寫看

提醒對方曾經答應過你在某個日期前給你回音

☞ During the interview, you mentioned that I would be informed of the result of my application before June 30th. It's already July 7th, but I haven't heard any information from you. I'm sending this letter to show my ambition and interest in this position and hopefully you can reconsider my application.

在面試時，您有提到會在6月30日前通知我應徵的結果。但今天已經是7月7日，我還沒收到您的回覆。我寫信來展現我對這份職務的抱負與興趣，希望您能重新考慮我的應徵案。

重申自己適合這份職務，展現企圖心，期盼對方可以主動和自己聯絡

☞ I am very eager to work in your company. I strongly believe I am the best man for this position since I have thorough knowledge of the field and have accumulated practical hands-on experiences. Please don't hesitate to contact me for further information. I hope I can be reconsidered for this job.

我很期待能在貴公司工作。我也相信以我對這領域的通盤知識和過去累積的實務經驗，讓我成為這份工作的最佳人選。請不吝和我聯繫，讓我能提供您更多的資料。希望我的應徵能再次被考慮。

其他詢問面談結果的萬用句

1. I'm sending this letter to ask if you have further questions regarding my application, and your timely consideration would be highly appreciated.

   我寫信來詢問您是否對於我的應徵有其他的問題，您若能及時考慮我的應徵，本人將感激不盡。

2. I'm writing to inquire the outcome of my interview last Friday. I'm very anxious to know your answer, and your prompt reply would be highly appreciated.

   我寫信來詢問有關上週五面試的結果。我很急著想要知道您的答案。若您能盡快回覆，我將十分感激。

3. I really enjoyed talking to you regarding this position during the interview. As I recall, you mentioned you would be getting back to me regarding the outcome before June 30th. Now the date has passed, and I'm wondering if you have made a decision for the position.

   我在面談時和您聊得很愉快。我記得您提到過會在6月30日前和我聯繫告知面試結果。但現在日期已經過了，我想知道您是否已經針對這個職務做了決定。

4. Thank you again for your time and consideration of my application. Please feel free to contact me once the final decisions are made regarding this position.

   謝謝您寶貴的時間與考慮我的應徵。若您做好決定，歡迎與我聯絡。

句型解說在這裡

句型

S + contribute to + n. / V-ing　　對……作出貢獻；捐款
S + contribute + O + to + n. / V-ing

- This professor has contributed a lot to the research of cure for AIDS.
  這位教授對於愛滋病解藥的研究貢獻良多。
- He has contributed a lot to raising these adopted children.
  他對扶養這些認養的孩子貢獻很多。
- The millionaire contributed half of his savings to charities.
  這位百萬富翁將他一半的積蓄捐給慈善團體。

所有格代名詞

	所有格形容詞 + 名詞	= 所有格代名詞
我的	my + n.	= mine
你（們）的	your + n,	= yours
他的	his + n.	= his
她的	her + n.	= hers
它的	its + n.	= its
我們的	our + n.	= ours
他們的	their + n.	= theirs

常見「所有格代名詞」使用時機：代換句子前半段提到的名詞
1. 比較級的前後名詞
   My car is better than yours (= your car). 我的車比你的（車）來的好。
2. a + n. + of +所有格代名詞
   He is a friend of mine (= my friends). 他是我的一個朋友。

練習時間試試看

詢問面試結果

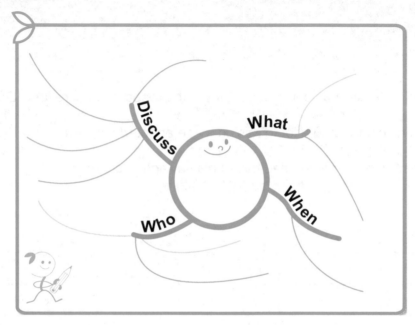

Step 1　Who are you writing to?

Step 2　What position you are applying for?

Step 3　When did you have an interview with the interviewer?

Step 4　What did you discuss in the interview?

練習範例分享

Dear Ms. Erwin,

Thank you so much for offering me an interview two weeks ago for the position of the executive assistant. I'm eager to work in your company and I sincerely believe I can be a great asset for this position.

However, I haven't received any reply from you regarding the outcome of your decision so far. I'm writing this letter to display my strong ambition and desire for this position and hope to hear from you as soon as possible.

Thank you again for your time and your reconsideration will be highly appreciated.

Sincerely,
Bill Jackson

對象

何時

內容

Erwin女士您好：

感謝您兩週前給我機會面試行政助理一職。我很希望能在貴公司工作，相信自己可以對此職務有所貢獻。

但到現在我還沒收到您的面試結果的決定。我寫信來展現我對這個職務的抱負與想望，希望能盡速得到您的回覆。

再次謝謝您寶貴的時間，若您能再考慮一下我的應徵，將十分感激。

Bill Jackson 敬上

Unit 8

業務

情境一
約定拜訪時間

情境二
詢問合作機會

情境三
確認訂單內容

情境一　約定拜訪時間

心智圖解說

約定
拜訪時間

When
Friday's meeting
this Monday's trade fair

Why
make a presentation

What
make an appoionment

Schedule
the customer's convenience

Who
Mr. Lo
Ms. Liang
Mr. Josh Thomas

寫作技巧錦囊

Step 1　Who are you writing to?　寫給誰
→ Mr. Josh Thomas

Step 2　What is this email for?　主旨
→ Business Appointment Letter: to make an appointment

Step 3　When did you last contact?　最後何時接觸
→ This Monday's trade fair

Step 4　Why do you want to make a business appointment?　面談原因
→ make a presentation

Step 5　Schedule a meeting date / time　約面談時間
→ to suit the customer's availability / convenience

單字片語搶先看

1. **trade fair** 商展；貿易展
   - These company representatives exchange their business cards at the trade fair.

   這些公司的代表在商展上彼此交換名片。

2. **be in business** 營業
   - This furniture retailer has been in business for decades.

   這間家具零售商已經營業幾十年了。

3. **transaction** *n.[C]* 交易；業務；買賣
   - The bank charges a fixed rate for each transaction.

   銀行會對每一筆交易收取固定的手續費。

4. **be acquainted with** 對……熟悉 *(= be familiar with)*
   - She's well acquainted with the process of visa application.

   她對於簽證申請流程很熟悉。

5. **pay someone a visit** 拜訪某人 *(=visit)*
   - May I pay you a visit tomorrow morning to offer free sampling session of our yogurt?

   我可以明天拜訪您提供優格的免費試吃活動嗎？

6. **demonstrate** *vi. vt.* 示威；展示
   - The sales representative is demonstrating the company's new tablet computer.

   這位業務代表正在示範操作該公司最新的平板電腦。

7. **associate** *n.[C]* 合夥人
   - One of his business associates ran away with millions of dollars.

   他的一位合夥人捲款數百萬逃走了。

英文範例

【★可替換其他面訪情境】

對象：旅行社

Dear Mr. Thomas,

→ 對象

★ I would like you to know how much I enjoyed talking to you on Monday's trade fair. And I'm very delighted to know our company's latest surveillance software, No Leak, has made a great impression. Transparent Technologies Inc. has been in business for more than 30 years developing high-tech software for office usages. No Leak is indeed the best security software ever developed to protect valuable customer information and transaction data.

→ 最後何時接觸

To make you acquainted with this software, I'm wondering if we can have a business meeting, so I can pay you a visit to further demonstrate to you and your associates how this software works.

→ 主旨

→ 面談原因

It would be our pleasure to meet you at your convenience. Please kindly suggest the appointment time. Feel free to contact me at 4556346260 or drop me email at faltu@zalaltu.com.

→ 約面談時間

I am looking forward to having a chance to meet you again.

Yours truly,

Allen B Bennett

段落大意

寒喧簡介	開場提醒上次曾見面或談話，點出自己公司和對方興趣的主力商品。
邀約面談	熱情提出希望見面進一步介紹商品或提供服務。
感謝與懇請回覆	要求對方回覆確認約面試時間。
信尾	客套語 + 署名。

中文翻譯

Thomas 先生您好，

我想讓您知道我在星期一的商展上和您相談甚歡。我很開心本公司最新的監視軟體No Leak讓您留下很好的印象。本公司Transparent科技已經在業界30餘年，發展辦公室用高科技軟體。而No Leak是我們所開發最棒的資料保全軟體，可以保護重要的客戶資料和交易資訊。

為了讓您更熟悉這一套軟體，我想詢問是否我們可以約個商業訪談，讓我可以拜訪您，進一步向您和您的合夥人展示如何使用這套軟體。

若能在您有空的時間跟您見面，將是我們的榮幸。請建議面訪時間。歡迎與我電話聯繫，電話號碼是4556346260或回傳電子郵件，電郵地址是faltu@zalatu.com。

期待有機會和您再見面。

Allen B Bennett 敬上

換個對象寫寫看

已約好會面時間：再次確認或提醒時間，並提供會議資料

This letter is in response to the telephonic conversation we had last Saturday regarding our business meeting. I am writing to confirm our appointment on 15th February at 4:00 pm in your office, in which I will make a presentation to demonstrate our marketing campaign proposal for your latest cosmetics. Please go through the enclosed proposal and suggest if any changes are required.

這封信是回應上週六我們在電話裡討論要約商務會議。我寫信來確認會議時間是2月15日下午4點在您的辦公室，會議上我會做簡報，展示我們為推廣貴公司化妝品所設計的行銷企劃案。請先過目附件的企劃案內容，並指出是否有需要修正之處。

與客戶從新業務開發信函（介紹公司及產品，邀約回信）

For superior and dependable shipping service, the world turns to Reeco, International. With a recently expanded fleet of larger ships and new state-of-the-art refrigerated containers, Reeco, International can handle the most demanding shipping challenges. A world standard for customer service is just a click away. Click "I'd like to learn more." to reply this email so our regional representatives can schedule a meeting with you.

想要優越可靠的貨運服務，所有人都會找Reeco國際。我們有最新擴大的船隻艦隊和獨步全球的冷凍櫃，讓本公司可以應付最艱鉅的運輸挑戰。現在這樣世界級的服務客戶和你只有一個按鍵的距離。點選「我想要知道更多詳情」回覆此信，我們的地區代表就能和您聯繫安排拜訪時間。

其他約面談時間的萬用語

I'm writing to make an appointment with you for next Monday.
我寫信來和您約下週一面談。

I wonder if it would be convenient to meet you tomorrow.
我想問如果明天和您會面是否方便。

Would it be convenient if I pay you a visit this Friday afternoon?
本週五下午去拜訪您是否方便？

句型解說在這裡

句型1

A + make / leave / create + a + adj. + impression + on B
A給B留下……的印象

- This interviewee made a good impression on the employer.
  這位面試者給雇主留下不錯的印象。

延伸觀念

B have a + adj. + impression + of + A　　B對A的印象……

- The employer had a good impression of the interviewee.
  雇主對這位面試者的印象不錯。

sb. + have the impression that + 子句　　人印象中認為……

- Most people have the impression that products made in China must be in poor quality.
  大部分的人印象中覺得中國大陸製作的產品品質一定很差。

句型2

S is the + 最高級 + (that) + have / has + p.p　主詞……是……過最……
S is the + 最高級 + (that) S + have / has ever + p.p → that子句接
主動語態

- This is the best movie (that) I have ever seen.
  這是我看過最棒的電影。

S is the + 最高級 + ever + p.p → that子句接被動語態，只保留過去分詞

- This is the best software ever developed.
  這是被開發過最棒的軟體。
  = This is the best software that has ever been developed.

練習時間試試看

約定拜訪時間

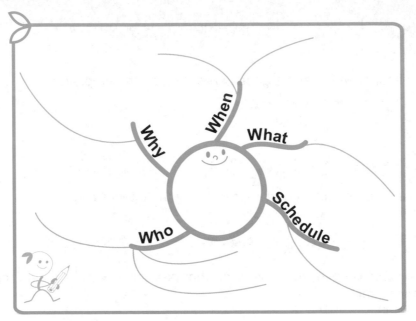

 Who are you writing to?　對象

 What is this email for?　主旨

 When did you last contact?　最後何時接觸

 Why do you want to make a business appointment?　面談原因

 Schedule a meeting / date / time　約面談時間

練習範例分享

【★可替換其他面訪情境】

Dear Ms. Lai,

★ I enjoyed talking to you on Monday's meeting and was very excited to know your company will launch a new line of jewelry in 3 months and is in need for marketing campaigns. I'm very pleased to inform you that our company has been in business for more than 15 years, providing brand marketing strategies. We're very confident that our experiences in event organizing and public relations can assist in enhancing brand awareness and boosting customer loyalty.

對象
最後何時接觸

To make you acquainted with our services, I'm wondering if we can have a business meeting to discuss in on the partnership. I'm wondering if you can squeeze in some time next Tuesday. Please feel free to contact me at 271564652 or email me at greatimpression@yahoo.com.

面談原因
主旨
約面談時間

I am looking forward to meeting you.

Yours truly,
Melody Chen

賴小姐您好，

在星期一的會議上和您相談甚歡。我很開心知道貴公司再過3個月要發表最新系列的珠寶，且正需要宣傳活動。我很榮幸要跟您說本公司已經在業界15年，提供品牌行銷策略。我們有信心我們在活動策劃以及公關活動上的經驗可以協助增加品牌識別度和顧客忠誠度。

為了讓您更熟悉我們的服務，我想詢問是否我們可以約個商業訪談，討論合作計畫，我想知道下週二您是否可以空出時間。歡迎與我電話聯繫，電話是271564652或回電子郵件，電郵地址是greatimpression@yahoo com。

期待有機會和您見面。

Melody 陳 敬上

情境二　詢問合作機會

心智圖解說

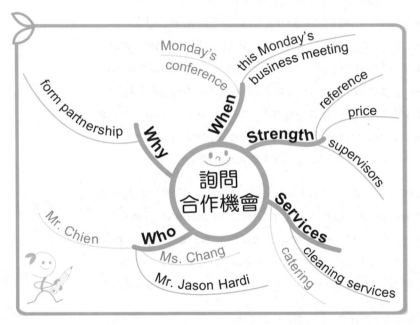

Monday's conference

this Monday's business meeting

When

form partnership

Why

reference

price

Strength

supervisors

詢問
合作機會

Services

cleaning services

catering

Mr. Chien

Who

Ms. Chang

Mr. Jason Hardi

寫作技巧錦囊

Who are you writing to?　對象
→ Mr. Jason Hardi

What services / products do you offer?　提供的服務
→ provide cleaning services for hotels or office complex

When and how did you last contact?　最後何時接觸
→ this Monday's business meeting

Why do you write this email?　寫信原因
→ form partnership

What's the strength of your product / services?　產品特色
→ high quality at low price, supervisors, list of reference

單字片語搶先看

1. look over 檢視 *(= check)*
   - The supervisor looked over my proposal and gave me some instructions for revision.
   主管檢視過我的企劃案並給我修改的指示。

2. ensure *vt.* 確保 *(= make sure)*
   - I double checked my resume to ensure there's no grammatical or spelling errors.
   我反覆檢查我的履歷，確保沒有文法或拼字錯誤。

3. technique *n.[C]* 技術
   - They have state-of-the-art techniques in renovating buildings.
   他們有高超的技術翻修建築物。

4. on a⋯⋯basis 以⋯⋯的頻率
   - My professor discusses with me regarding my thesis on a regular basis.
   我的指導教授定期和我討論我的論文。

5. client *n.[C]* 客戶 *(= customer)*
   - I'm a regular client of this finedining restaurant.
   我是這家高檔餐廳的常客。

6. stop by 順道拜訪
   - I'll stop by Uncle Sam and bring him your regards.
   我會順道拜訪山姆叔叔並代你向他問候。

7. contract *n.[C]* 合約
   - I had a lawyer look into all terms of the contract before signing it.
   我在簽署合約前請一位律師看過所有條約內容。

英文範例

詢問合作機會　　　　　　　　　　【★可代換其他尋求合作的可能】

Dear Mr. Hardi,　　　　　　　　　　　　　　　　　● 對象

Thank you very much for letting me meet with you and
your associates on Monday. I hope you have had time　　● 最後何時接觸
to look over our proposal to provide cleaning services
for Linslade Office Complex which I brought you on　　　● 提供的服務
Monday.

As I mentioned when we met, we take extra care to
ensure that your office suites receive the finest services
possible at reasonable costs. Our team of supervisors
constantly evaluate the products and techniques that
we use and inspect the work done by our cleaning
staff. What's more, they check with your office tenants
on a monthly basis to make sure the work is being
done to their satisfaction. Please feel free to check
anyone on the list I provide you with. I'm certain that all
our corporate clients are pleased with our work.　　　　● 產品特色

★ I'd like to stop by with a contract this Friday if　　　● 寫信原因
possible, so that we can start brightening the office
environment the Linslade Office Complex on the
first of next month.

Looking forward to be at your service soon.

Sincerely yours,
Sandy Chih

段落大意

| 寫信致謝 | 開場先感謝對方給予面談合作的機會。 |

| 公司與產品強項 | 強調給客戶的產品或服務優勢。 |

| 敬請回覆 | 要求對方收到訊息後回覆。 |

| 信尾 | 客套語 ＋ 署名。 |

中文翻譯

Hardi先生您好：

謝謝您讓我週一有機會可以和您以及您的合夥人面談。希望您已經先過目過我當天帶給您看的合作企劃案，瞭解我們可以為貴商務大樓提供的清掃服務。

就如我當天會晤時所提到的，我們用心確保辦公大樓各樓房都能以合理的花費獲得最好的清潔服務。我們的監督團隊時常評估我們使用的產品和技術，以及巡視清潔人員的作業。此外，他們也會每月和貴大樓的住戶確認他們滿意我們的清潔品質。我附上一份用戶推薦名單，歡迎您和名單上的用戶聯繫。我確信所有和我們合作過的客戶都很滿意我們的品質。

如果可以的話，我想要本週五到貴公司一趟給您一份合約書，這樣我們最快下個月一號就可以開始為貴辦公大樓打掃環境了。

希望能盡快為您服務。

Sandy齊　敬上

換個對象寫寫看

附上合約，再約見面討論合約的細節

- Please find enclosed a copy of the contract for your reference. If possible, I'd like to schedule another meeting with you to discuss the contract and see if we agree with all the terms and conditions. We look forward to building partnership with you and I'm certain you will be pleased with our services.

  請參考所附上的合約書。如果可能的話，我想要跟您再約個時間見面討論合約，確認我們是否同意裡面所有的條約。我很希望能和您建立合作關係，也相信您一定會滿意我們的服務。

詢問合作企劃考慮的如何

- During our previous meeting, I've brought about the proposal regarding future partnership. We are confident that your company will be pleased with our services / products and the proposal will bring mutual benefits. It would be appreciated if you can consider the proposal and decide to cooperate with our company.

  在我們上一的會談中，我提出了未來合作的企劃案。我們很有信心貴公司會對我們的服務或產品感到滿意，這個合作企劃案也會帶來互惠。您若能考慮我們的提案並和我們公司合作，將感激不盡。

其他詢問有無合作可能萬用語

- It would be our pleasure to be at your service.
  若能為您服務，將是我們的榮幸。
- I'm writing this letter to inquire your feedback and comments on the proposal for mutual cooperation.
  我寫信來詢問您對於雙方合作企劃案的回應。
- Please don't hesitate to contact me regarding any questions in the terms and conditions of the contract.
  若您對於合約細節有任何疑問，請不吝與我聯繫。
- I have faith that we can form a successful business partnership, and any of your suggestion and comments are welcome as to how we can cooperate.
  我相信我們一定可以共創成功的合作關係，歡迎提出任何對於如何合作的建議和想法。

句型解說在這裡

句型1

A + let B + VR　　A讓B做……

☞ The parents won't let their daughter go on a date alone.
這對父母不讓她們的女兒單獨出外約會。

延伸句型

使役動詞

A + have / make + B + VR　　＝A要求命令B去做
A + ask / tell / get + B + to V

☞ Mom made me sweep the floor last night. 媽媽昨晚叫我掃地。
= Mom asked me to sweep the floor last night.

句型2

at a……cost　　以……的花費

☞ You can get a chic haircut at a very reasonable cost.
你可以以合理的價錢剪一頭流行的髮型。

延伸觀念

at + 時間／速度／價錢／代價

☞ You can enjoy fine dining at a very affordable price at this restaurant.
在這間餐廳你可以用負擔得起的價格吃到精緻的餐點。
☞ A high-speed camera can capture any movement at the speed of light.
高速攝影機可以以光速的速度捕捉任何的動作。

練習時間試試看

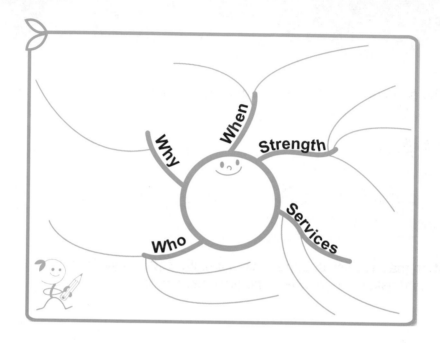

Step 1　Who are writing to?　對象？

Step 2　What services / products do you offer?　提供的服務？

Step 3　When and how did you last contact?　最後何時接觸？

Step 4　Why do you write this email?　寫信原因？

Step 5　What's the strength of your product / services?　產品特色？

練習範例分享

Dear Ms. Anderson,   ● 對象

Thank you very much for letting me meet with you on
Monday. I am very excited to learn that you are opening   ● 最後何時接觸
more English teaching institutes all over Taiwan and
is in need of fast and reliable services for recruiting
qualified teachers.

A lot of ESL schools feel that finding a good teacher
is difficult. This is where we at Reach and Teach
come in. Our motto is matching great teachers with
great schools. We carefully screen all job applicants   ● 提供的服務
to ensure our teachers possess satisfactory teaching
qualifications and skills.
                                                         ● 產品特色
I have faith that we can form a successful business
partnership, and please kindly reply to this email and
tell me what you think about the proposal we brought
you on Monday.
                                                         ● 寫信原因
Looking forward to hearing from you soon.
Sincerely yours,
Claire Wen

Anderson女士您好：

謝謝您讓我週一有機會可以和您面談。我很高興得知您計畫要在全臺灣開設更多語
言教學機構，且需要快速可靠的師資仲介服務。
很多語言學校發現要找到好老師是很困難的，而這就是我們Reach and Teach公司切
入協助的部分。我們的座右銘是就幫好老師找到好的學校。我們細心審查每位求職
者的背景，確保我們仲介的老師都有令人滿意的教學背景或技巧。
我相信我們可以建立很成功的合作關係。請回覆此郵件讓我知道您對於周一我們帶
去的企劃案的想法。
希望能盡快得到您的回音。

Claire 溫　敬上

情境三　確認訂單內容

心智圖解說

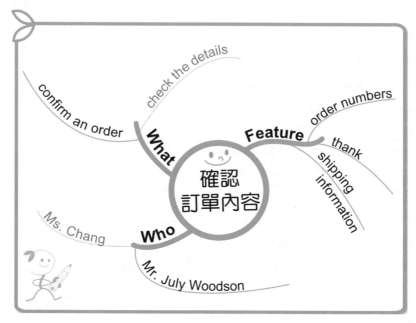

寫作技巧錦囊

Who are writing to?　對象？
→ Mr. July Woodson

What is this email for?　主旨？
→ confirm an order

features in your email confirmation　內容？
→ thank the customer for the order, order number, shipping information

單字片語搶先看

1. location *n.[C]* 位置
   - The hotel is situated in a perfect location overlooking the lake.
     這間旅館位置絕佳，眺望整個湖景。

2. method *n.[C]* 方式 *(= way, means)*
   - There are various payment methods to choose from when you shop online.
     在網路上購物，有多種付款方式可供選擇。

3. within 在……之內
   - I demand the products to be delivered within three days of order.
     我要求貨品在下訂後三天內送達。

4. business day 工作天
   - The customer service staff will contact me within two business days.
     克服人員會在兩個工作天內和我聯繫。

5. sub-total 小計
   - The sub-total amount doesn't include shipping fees or taxes.
     小計的費用不包含運費和稅。

6. parcel *n.[C]* 包裹
   - The parcel arrived in two days after I made the order.
     包裹在我訂貨後兩天送達。

7. bill *n.[C]* 帳單；票據
   - The billing address is the same as the shipping address.
     發票寄送地址和收貨地址一樣。

英文範例

【★可增加其他訂單確認細節】

確認訂單內容

Dear Ms. Woodson,

Thank you for shopping at xyz.com. Depending on your location and shipping method, you should receive your product(s) within 3 to 5 business days after we confirm your payment. — 對象

★ Order Number: 10320

Order Date: Friday 27 February, 2013

Payment Method: Secure Credit Card

Products

2 x Long-sleeved Wool Sweater (L, Purple) $19.98 / each

Sub-Total: $39.96

United Parcel Service (shipping fee): $11.42

Total: $51.38

Shipping Address:

No 123 Pine St.

New York, NY 10001

United States

Billing Address:

Same as the above — 內容

Please confirm this order and make the payment at your earliest convenience. — 主旨

Sincerely,

Andy Curton

段落大意

| 寫信目的 | 開場先說明感謝對方下訂單。 |

| 細節 | 訂單品項等細節確認。 |

| 敬請回覆 | 請求對方收到訊息後儘快回覆確認並付款。 |

| 信尾 | 客套語 + 署名。 |

中文翻譯

Woodson小姐您好：

謝謝您在XYZ網站上下訂單。根據您的送貨地址和運輸方式，您會在我們收到費用後3到5個工作天內收到您訂購的商品。
訂單代號：10320
訂貨日期：2013年2月27日
付款方式：安全的信用卡
訂購商品明細：
2件長袖羊毛毛衣（L尺碼，紫色）單件價格19.98美元
小計：39.96美元
聯邦貨運服務（運費）11.42美元
總計：51.38美元
送貨地址：松樹街123號，紐約，美國，區域號碼10001
發票地址：同上
請確認以上訂單無誤，並請您盡快付費。

Andy Curton　敬上

換個對象寫寫看

提供免付費電話或訂單查詢服務

○ Your satisfaction is important to us, so if you have any questions please don't hesitate to email or call us toll free at 0800-123-123. When contacting us about this order, please be sure to include your order number. You may track the progress of this order by logging onto http: / / www. xyz.com /

您的滿意度對我們來說很重要，所以如果您有任何問題，歡迎回信給我們或撥打免付費電話0800123123。與我們聯繫討論訂單內容時，請務必給予訂單代號。您也可以進入以下網址http: / / www.xyz.com / 查詢訂單處理狀況。

告知客戶已經收到貨款，正在出貨中

○ We also received the payment of US51.38 in form of ATM transaction on Feb 28th. The items are being sent to the address as mentioned in the letter of order. The items are expected to be delivered on within the 5 or 6 days of receipt of orders. The statement of orders and bill along with the warranty documents will be delivered along with the items.

我們也已經在2月28日收到您ATM轉帳的51.38美金貨款。您所訂購的商品正在出貨到收貨地址。預計在我們收到訂單後5到6個工作天送達。訂單明細、帳單、以及保固文件也會跟著貨品一併送達。

其他訂單確認信件會有的句子

○ We are thankful to for the order and pleased to serve you. We hope that your association with us will continue in the future also.

我們很感謝您的訂單，也很榮幸能為您服務。希望您未來也能繼續向我們訂貨。

○ Any defects in the items or any problems with the statement of orders must be reported at the earliest.

任何商品的瑕疵或訂單明細的問題請盡速和我們反應。

○ The invoice is enclosed, along with an order form for next year's catalog. We sincerely hope you can continue utilizing our services.

附上發票，以及明年型錄和訂單。我們竭誠歡迎您能持續使用我們的服務。

句型解說在這裡

句型1

depend on　　由……決定

○ Whether the outdoor barbecue will held depends on the weather.
室外烤肉是否會舉辦由天候決定。

延伸句型

depend on / rely on / count on　　依賴

○ Children depend on their parents for food and shelter.
孩子依賴父母取得食物和庇護。

句型2

the same as……　和……一樣

○ My cell phone is the same as yours.
我的手機和你的一樣。

延伸句型

the same + N + as……

○ My cell phone has the same features as yours.
我的手機和你的功能一樣。

練習時間試試看

確認訂單內容

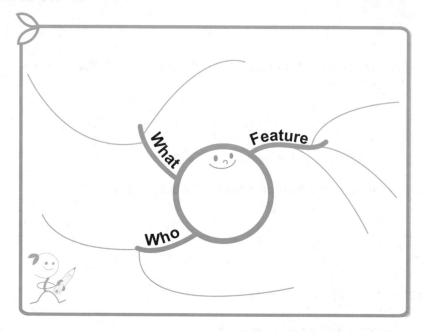

 Who are writing to?　對象

 What is this email for?　主旨

 Features in your email confirmation　內容

練習範例分享

Dear Ms. Chen,

對象

Thank you for shopping at easybuy.com. We have received your purchase order for the following.
Order Number: 105200
Order Date: Friday 27 February, 2013
2 X microwave oven NT$3500 / each
1 X washing machine NT$15000 / each

Sub-Total: $22000
Shipping Service (ground): NT$700

Total: $22700

Payment Method: Credit Card
Shipping Address:
2F，No 25 Ming Chuang East Road, Taipei City

Billing Address:
Same as the above

內容

Please confirm this order and make the payment within three days of orders. The products are expected to be delivered within 5 business days after confirmation of payment.

主旨

Sincerely,
Jennifer Wu

陳小姐您好：

謝謝您在easybuy網站上下訂單。我們已收到以下您的訂單。
訂單代號：105200
訂貨日期：2013年2月27日
付款方式：安全的信用卡
訂購商品明細：
2台微波爐 單品價格3500台幣
1台洗衣機 單品價格15000台幣
小計：22000台幣
貨運服務(運送到一樓) 700台幣
總計：22700台幣
送貨地址：台北市民權東路25號2樓
發票地址：同上
請確認以上訂單無誤，並請您在三日內付費。貨品會在確認收到貨款後5個工作天內送達。

Jennifer 吳 敬上

Unit 9

採購

情境一
詢價

情境二
以量制價

情境三
確認交易

情境一　詢價

心智圖解說

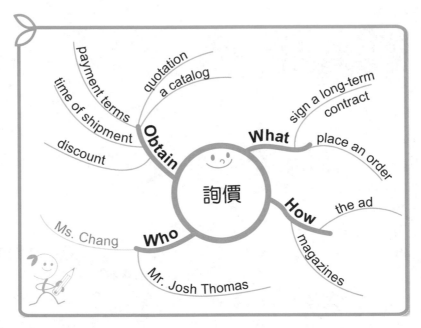

payment terms
quotation
a catalog
time of shipment
Obtain
discount

sign a long-term contract
What
place an order

詢價

How
the ad
magazines

Ms. Chang
Who
Mr. Josh Thomas

寫作技巧錦囊

 Step 1
Who is the thank-you note for?　對象？
→ Mr. Josh Thomas

 Step 2
How did you hear of the company / product?　如何得知？
→ the ad on newspaper, magazines

 Step 3
What do you want to obtain?　希望獲得的資訊？
→ a catalog, quotation, request for an offer, time of shipment, discount

 Step 4
What will you do if you can accept the quotation / offer?（將來發展）
→ place an order, sign a long-term contract

單字片語搶先看

1. **manufacturer** *n.[C]* 製造商
   - The manufacturer of organic cosmetics dedicates to using organic natural materials.
   這個有機化妝品製造商致力於使用有機的天然材料。
   詞類變化：manufacture *vt. vi* 製造.

2. **catalog** *n.[C]* 型錄
   - This catalog fully illustrates the medical benefit of the herbal tea.
   這個型錄充分說明這款花草茶的醫療功效。

3. **quotation** *n.[C]* 報價
   - May I have the lowest quotation of your products?
   我可不可以請您針對產品給我最優惠的報價？
   詞類變化：quote vi. vt. 引用

4. **term** *n.[C]* 條款
   - Both companies are still negotiating regarding the terms in the contract.
   兩個公司對於合約條款還在研討中。

5. **discount** *n.[C,U]* 折扣；打折扣
   - I can get a discount if I buy in large quantities.
   如果我大量購買可以享有優惠。

6. **supply** *vt.* 提供 *(=offer, provide)*
   - I'm wondering if the manufacturer can supply products in large quantities.
   我想知道製造商是否可以大量供貨。

7. **sample** *n.[C]* 試用品；樣品
   - You can try the sample first before you decide whether to make a purchase.
   在決定是否購買之前你可以先試用樣品。

英文範例

詢價

【★可替換其他詢價內容】

Dear Mr. Thomas,

We are the manufacturer of instant coffee powder. Your

ad of coffee beans on Money Daily interests us. ★

We'd like to receive the latest catalog of all your coffee

beans and powder, as well as the details of the lowest

quotation you can offer and the terms of payment.

Please quote us your best offer for coffee beans per

kilogram and the discount you can allow. We will

also find it more helpful if you can supply samples. In

addition, we'd like to inquire if we can purchase online.

I am looking forward to having from you soon,

Yours truly,

Juliet Browning

對象

如何得知

希望獲得資訊

段落大意

寫信目的	開場自我介紹，點出對該公司產品有興趣，想要詢價。
請教細節	請對方具體報價，提供型錄、樣品、折扣及付款方式等細節。
敬請回覆	要求對方回覆確認報價。
信尾	客套語 + 署名。

中文翻譯

Thomas先生您好，

我們是即溶咖啡粉製造商。我們對您在金錢日報上的咖啡豆廣告很感興趣，我們想取得你們最新的咖啡豆和咖啡粉產品型錄，以及您能提供最優惠的報價和付款說明等細節。

請給我們每公斤咖啡豆的最低報價，以及你們可以提供的折扣。若您能提供樣品，那就更有幫助了。此外，我們也想詢問是否可以在網路上訂購。

期待盡快收到您的回覆。

Juliet Browning 敬上

換個對象寫寫看

需從海外進口的物品

◦ Please send us the quotation per kilogram C&F Taipei, Taiwan, including insurance, handling, and freight. We'd also like to know the minimum export quantities and the time of shipment.
請給我們貨物運到台灣台北的到貨價，包含保險，手續費和運費。我們也想要詢問出口最低進貨量，以及貨運時間。

提醒最晚報價期限

◦ Since we have already made an inquiry of all your articles, would you please make an offer by the end of this week? We'd like to know the prices (exclusive of tax) of all your products.
既然我們已經向您的產品詢價過，可否請您能在本週末前給我們不含稅的報價？

其他詢價的萬用句型

◦ Please quote us the lowest price for all the items listed hereunder.
請針對以下品項給我們最低的報價。
◦ I'd like to have your lowest offer / quotations for the ink cartridge.
我想要知道您們墨水匣的最低報價。
◦ Prices quoted should include freight to Taiwan and insurance.
報價請包含到台灣的運費以及保險。
◦ Please keep us informed of the latest quotation of the following articles.
請告知我們以下品項的最新報價。
◦ We would highly appreciate it if you can forward the latest samples along with best prices.
若您能附上最新的樣品以及最優惠的報價，我們將非常感激。
◦ Please also inform me how this offer remains firm / open.
也請告知這個報價有效期間有多長。
◦ Full / Detailed information regarding prices, quality, quantity available and other particulars would be very appreciated.
若能詳列價格、品質、供貨數量以及其他條件，將會讓我十分感激。

句型解說在這裡

句型1

A + 單音節形容詞-er + than B 比較級

more + 多音節形容詞

- The blue box is bigger than the yellow box.
  這個藍色的盒子比黃色的盒子大。
- A computer is more expensive than a bicycle.
  電腦比腳踏車貴。

句型觀念

比較的對象要同性質

- Your pencil is longer than mine.(= my pencil.)
  你的筆比我（的筆）長。
- The weather in Taiwan is hotter than that (= the weather) in Japan.
  台灣的天氣比日本（的天氣）熱。
- People in Kaohsiung are more generous than those (= people) in Taipei.
  高雄人比台北（人）熱情。

句型2

A + be + the 單音節形容詞-est + in 地區 / of 團體 最高級

the most + 多音節形容詞

- The elephant is the biggest animal in the zoo.
  大象是動物園裡最大的動物。
- This one is the most expensive of all the cars in the store.
  這部車是店裡最貴的一輛。

練習時間試試看

詢價

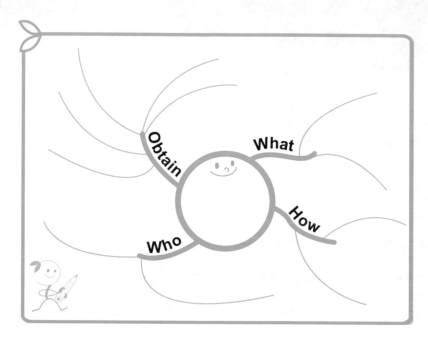

 Who are you writing to? 對象

 How did you hear of the company / product? 如何得知

 What do you want to obtain? 希望獲得的資訊

 What will you do if you can accept the quotation / offer? 將來發展

練習範例分享

Dear Sir or Madam,

I'm in charge of purchasing air conditioners for all our
school classrooms, and I'm interested in buying in
large quantity with you directly. We'd like to get the
latest catalog of all models available, with detailed
description of features and prices. And please make
the best offer and discount you can allow since we will
purchase about 32 to 35 air conditioners.
We'd also like to know if you can provide free shipping
and free installation services of the air conditioners. In
addition, can we pay in 24-month installments with 0%
interest rate?
If the prices, quality of products and services are
acceptable, we will consider purchasing in large quantity.
Hope to hear from you soon,

Yours truly,
Peter Cruise

對象

如何得知

希望獲得資訊

希望獲得資訊

將來發展

敬啟者：
我負責採買我們學校所有教室的冷氣，對於直接和您大宗採購很有興趣。請提供我們您所有機種的型錄，要有詳細的性能說明和報價。既然我們會大宗採購32到35台冷氣，請給我最優惠的價格和折扣。
我們也想知道您是否提供免費冷氣運送和安裝服務。此外，我們是否可以24期零利率分期付款？
如果價格，品質和服務都可以接受，我們就會考慮大量訂購。
期待盡快收到您的回覆。

Peter Cruise 敬上

情境二　以量制價

心智圖解說

以量制價

- Why
  - long-term contract
  - pay in cash
  - large quantities
- What
  - counter offer
- Offer
  - payment terms
  - shipment
  - discount
  - quotation
  - samples
  - catalog
- What
  - 15% off
  - 10% off
- Who
  - Mr. Huang
  - Ms. Lee
  - Ms. Eileen Cooper

寫作技巧錦囊

Who are you writing to?　對象
→ Ms. Eileen Cooper

What is this email for?　主旨
→ counter offer

What did the other party **offer** you?　對方提供什麼
→ a catalog, quotation, payment terms, discount, samples

Why do you bargain for / negotiate the prices?　講價的原因
→ purchase in bulk / in large quantities, pay in cash, sign a long-term contract

What do your counter offer?　講價金額
→ 10% off the offered price

單字片語搶先看

1. acknowledge *vt.* 告知收到
   - ☞ I acknowledge receipt of her email.
     我有收到她的電子郵件。

2. in reply to 回應
   - ☞ I'm writing this letter in reply to your enquiry.
     我正在寫信回覆你的詢價。

3. offer *n.[C]* 報價
   - ☞ Thank you for making an offer but we've found it too high to accept.
     謝謝您報價,但我們覺得報價金額過高無法接受。

4. make some / an allowance 打折
   - ☞ That store makes an allowance of 10% for cash payment.
     這家商店對於現金付款再折價10%。

5. quoted *adj.* 報價的
   - ☞ We don't find the quoted prices competitive at all.
     我們不覺得您的報價有任何競爭力。

6. relationship *n.[C]* 關係 (+ with)
   - ☞ It's very important to maintain a stable relationship with your suppliers.
     和供應商保持穩定的關係很重要。

7. permanent *adj.* 永久的;長期的
   - ☞ You are offered an permanent position as a construction site supervisor.
     你得到了一個長期工地監工的職務。

英文範例

對象：旅行社　　　　　　　　　　【★可替換其他還價訴求】

Dear Ms. Cooper,

　　　　　　　　　　　　　　　　　　　　　　　　● 對象

We acknowledge receiving your quotations and

samples of all your lines of beverages. We appreciate

　　　　　　　　　　　　　　　　　　　　　　　　● 對方提供什麼

your prompt response.

★ In reply to your offer, we think the prices are higher

than expected. We'd like to know if you can make

some allowance, say 10% on the quoted prices of all

　　　　　　　　　　　　　　　　　　　　　　　　● 主旨

the drinks available, considering we will make purchase

　　　　　　　　　　　　　　　　　　　　　　　　● 講價金額

in large quantities each semester, and that our term of

payment is in cash.

　　　　　　　　　　　　　　　　　　　　　　　　● 講價原因

We sincerely hope to build a long-term business

relationship with you as our permanent drink supplier,

and we intend to sign a long-term contract if you can

consider our counter-offer favorably and let us have

your acceptance.

I am looking forward to having from you soon.

Yours Sincerely,

Bruce Wills

段落大意

寫信目的　開場感謝對方報價，但希望能再議價。

討價還價　說明自己大宗採購且支付現金，希望爭取更多折扣及優惠服務。

懇請回覆　要求對方回覆確認報價，希望對方提供優惠。

信尾　客套語 ＋ 署名。

中文翻譯

Cooper小姐您好，

我們已收到您所有系列飲料的報價和樣品。我們很感謝您即刻的回覆。

回應您的報價，我們覺得報價高於預期。我們想詢問您是否可以調降價格，給我們約報價10%的折扣，考慮到我們每學期都會大量訂購，以及考量到我們都以現金付款。

我們竭誠希望能和您建立長久的合作關係，讓您成為我們長期的飲料供應商，若您能考慮並接受我們的議價，我們甚至會計畫和您簽訂長期合約。

期待盡快收到您的回覆。

Bruce Wills敬上

換個對象寫寫看

對方報價比市場或比其他議價者高

☞ We very much regret to state we consider the prices out of line with the prevailing market level. Your quoted prices appear to be higher compared to those offered by other suppliers and we have other offers of similar items with much lower prices. To have the business concluded, we suggest the price be lowered by at least 10%.

我們很遺憾要告知您，我們覺得您的報價高於市場水準。您的報價和其他供應商的報價比起來也過高，我們得到的其他報價都比您的低很多。若要成交，我們建議您能降價至少10%。

對方報價讓自己沒有利潤空間

☞ We would like to take this opportunity to cooperate with you. However, the quoted prices are way too high, which will leave no margin of profit on our side, and it will be rather difficult to push any sales if we accept the prices as quoted. Could you please cut the prices by 10%, so to enable us to introduce your products to more customers?

我們很想利用這個機會和您合作。但您的報價過高，這會讓我們沒有利潤空間，若我們接受這個報價，將難以帶動銷售量。您是否可以給個10%的折扣，讓我們可以介紹您的產品給更多顧客？

其他議價的萬用句型

☞ I'm afraid that your quoted prices are too high and thus we find it difficult to accept the offer.
我們認為您的報價太高，因此我們難以接受。

☞ We think we are eligible to obtain a substantial discount to your quoted price, considering we'll make bulk purchase.
我們認為我們有資格要求更多的折扣，考慮到我們會大宗採購。

☞ If you can quote us a 10% discount off your list price, we would very much appreciate it.
若你可以報給我們九折優惠，我們將會非常感激。

句型解說在這裡

句型1

比較級 than expected　　比預期來的……

- My telephone bill is higher than expected.
  我的電話帳單金額比我預期來的高。

句型觀念

比較級 than + adj.

- You've got more than necessary.
  你擁有的已經比需要的多很多了。
- He has performed better than anticipated.
  他比預期的表現好很多。

句型2

intend / attempt / plan to V　　打算／企圖／計畫去做.

- The entrepreneur intends to merger another company.
  這位企業家打算要併購另一家公司。
- The criminal attempted to escape the prison but failed.
  這名罪犯企圖越獄但卻失敗了。
- I have planned to go on working holiday in Australia this summer.
  我計畫今年暑假去澳洲度假打工。

練習時間試試看

以量制價

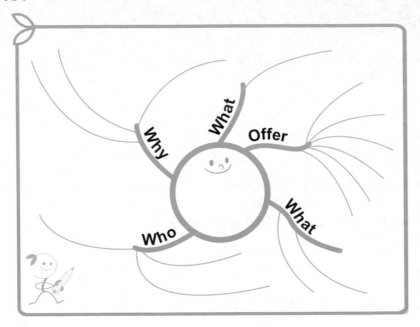

 Step 1 Who are you writing to? 對象

 Step 2 What is this email for? 主旨

 Step 3 What did the other party offer you? 對方提供什麼

 Step 4 Why do you bargain for / negotiate the prices? 講價的原因

 Step 5 What do you counter offer? 講價金額

練習範例分享

Dear Ms. Huckings,

對象

Thank you for your prompt quotations of printers in response to our enquiry.

對方提供什麼

However, we very much regret to tell you that we don't find the quoted price acceptable. We have obtained offers from other suppliers and all of them made more attractive offers. Since we will make bulk purchase of 50 printers, we expect more competitive prices from you.

主旨
講價原因

We're wondering if you could reduce the prices by 15% so you stand better chance of concluding the business.

講價金額

We sincerely hope to build a long-term business relationship with you if you can consider our counter-offer favorably and let us have your acceptance a.s.a.p.

Your prompt response will be much appreciated.

Sincerely,

Henry Millers

Huckings小姐您好,

感謝您迅速針對我們印表機的詢價作報價。

但很遺憾地,我們無法接受您的報價。我們有其他廠商的報價,價格都比你的來的有吸引力。既然我們會大量採購50台印表機,我們期待能從您這裡取得更有競爭力的報價。我們想詢問您是否可以調降價格15%,以便有更多機會可以成交。

若您能考慮並接受我們的議價,並盡速回應答應我們的提議,我們竭誠希望能和您建立長久的合作關係。

若您能盡快回覆,將感激不盡。

Henry Millers敬上

情境三　確認交易

心智圖解說

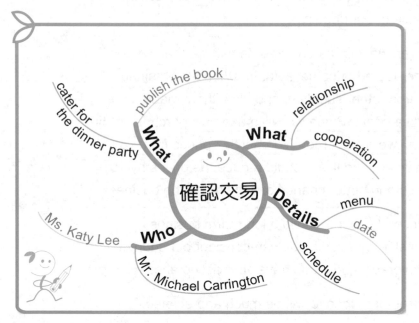

- publish the book
- cater for the dinner party
- **What**
- relationship
- **What**
- cooperation
- 確認交易
- **Details**
- menu
- date
- Ms. Katy Lee
- **Who**
- schedule
- Mr. Michael Carrington

寫作技巧錦囊

Step 1　**Who** are you writing to?　對象
→ Mr. Michael Carrington

Step 2　**What** is this email for?　主旨
→ relationship, cooperation

Step 3　**What** will the other party do for you?　對方為你做什麼
→ to cater for dinner party

Step 4　**Details** of the work / project　工作細節
→ menu, schedule

單字片語搶先看

1. **notes** *n.[C]* 筆記；紀錄 *(= records)*
   - The diligent student takes notes of every lecture he attends.
     這名用功的學生每場演講都會抄筆記。

2. **valuable** *adj.* 有價值的
   - This vase is valuable due to its unique designs.
     這個花瓶價值非凡因為它獨一無二的設計。

3. **appetizer** *n.[C]* 開胃菜
   - What's the appetizer for today's set?
     今日套餐的開胃菜是什麼？

4. **set up** 準備
   - The chef and his staff got up early to set up for the brunch.
     主廚和他的團隊起個大早準備早午餐。

5. **handle** *vi. vt.* 操作起來；處理
   - This experienced counselor can handle challenging interpersonal issues.
     這位經驗豐富的諮詢師可以處理極具挑戰性的人際相處課題。

6. **clean-up** 打掃清理
   - Mom enjoys the process of cooking but is not that into clean-up.
     媽媽很享受煮飯的過程但不是很喜歡清理。

7. **dining** *n.[U]* 用餐
   - There is no separate dining area in this apartment.
     這間公寓沒有獨立的用餐空間。

英文範例

Dear Mr. Carrington,　　　　　　　　　　　　　對象

I enjoyed meeting you last Friday. Your enthusiasm

for the menu for our Dec. 13 dinner meeting in the

Redwood is contagious. My mouth is already watering!　　對方為你做什麼

According to my notes, you will be preparing the

following for our 87 valuable guests:

Main course: Choice of chicken piccata or vegetarian　　工作細節

　　　　　　Medley Plus

Salad: Frensh spinach, mandarin orange, and almond　　工作細節

　　salad

Appetizer: Angel hair pasta with white clam sauce　　工作細節

Dessert: Raspberry and white chocolate tarts　　工作細節

Drink: Coffee or herbal tea　　工作細節

Also, your staff of ten will arrive at 4:30 p.m. for setting　　工作細節

up, serve the food at 7 p.m. and handle the clean-up.

The dinner will end no later than 10 p.m.

Please confirm the above details and don't hesitate to　　工作細節

contact me for any further questions.　　工作細節

Look forward to your high-quality dining services.

Yours truly,

Trudy Jolie

段落大意

寫信目的	開場感謝對方與您合作。
細節確認	條列出合作內容，具體提供細節。
懇請回覆	要求對方回覆確認，期待雙方合作愉快。
信尾	客套語 + 署名。

中文翻譯

Carrington先生您好，

很高興上週五和您會面。您為12月13日在紅木廳舉辦的晚宴設計菜單，您的熱情很有感染力，我早就口水直流了。

根據我的筆記，您為我們87位嘉賓準備以下佳餚：

主菜：雞肉捲餅或綜合蔬食。
再加上
沙拉：新鮮菠菜佐金桔杏仁沙拉
前菜：天使義大利細麵佐蛤蜊白醬
甜點：覆盆子白巧克力塔
飲料：咖啡或花草茶

此外，您的十人團隊會在4點半就位開始佈置會場，七點開始上餐，並處理後續的清潔與整理。晚宴會在十點前結束。
請確認以上細節，有任何疑問歡迎請與我聯繫。

期待享受您高品質的餐飲服務。

Trudy Jolie敬上

換個對象寫寫看

其他確認合作細節的萬用句型

表達感謝對方給予合作機會

- We are very delighted to have finally built business partnership with you.
  我們很開心終於和您建立了合作關係。

- Thank you for the opportunity to offer you high-quality products / services. We'll definitely do our best to exceed your expectations.
  謝謝您給我們機會讓我們提供您高品質的產品或服務。我們必全力以赴以超越您對我們的期待。

- I'd like to take this opportunity to express our gratitude of being at your service with our fantastic products / services.
  我想藉這個機會表達感謝之意，感謝您讓我們為您服務，提供您高品質的產品與服務。

提供合作細節請對方確認

- I have enclosed the notes / contract for all the details of the project. Would you please take some time to look into the terms or conditions of the contract and reply this email to confirm or report any changes or questions.
  我附上這個企劃案的細節／合約，請您花些時間過目所有條款或細節，並回覆確認或是回報任何您想做的修正或發現的問題。

- I have summarized all the details of our corporation in this project and please refer to the enclosed notes. It would be appreciated if you can read them thoroughly to confirm that you agree with all the terms and details.
  我已經摘要所有合作細節，請看附件的摘要紀錄。若您能詳細過目並確認同意所有條約和細節，我將感激不盡。

- Enclosed please read the details of responsibilities for both parties regarding the business partnership. Your confirmation of all matters will be much appreciated and please don't hesitate to point out any questions for further discussion or clarification.
  附件是我們雙方合作的工作細節，若您能確認所有細項，我們會感激不盡。也請不吝提出任何疑問，以便進一步討論或澄清。

重申本公司會遵守工作合約

- We will comply with all the terms and conditions listed in the contract.
  我們會遵守合約所有規定與條件。

- We will abide by all regulations and fulfill all the responsibilities we both agree with.
  我們會遵守所有規定並完成我們共同同意的工作內容。

句型解說在這裡

句型1

enjoy + V-ing　　喜歡去做……

- He enjoys listening to Korean pop songs.
  他喜歡聽韓國流行歌曲。

句型觀念

like / love + to V / V-ing = be into + V-ing / N = be fond of V-ing

- Jenny likes to play the piano. = Jenny likes playing the piano.
  Jenny喜歡彈鋼琴。
- He is into watching soap opera.
  他很喜歡看連續劇。
- He is fond of sharing photos on Facebook.
  他喜歡在臉書上分享照片。

句型2

prepare (O) for N　　為……準備……

- Mom is preparing dishes for the dinner party.
  媽媽正在為晚宴準備菜餚。

句型觀念

prepare for N　　為……作準備

- He is preparing for the college entrance exam.
  他正在準備大學入學考試。

prepare oneself for N　　為……做好準備

- You need to prepare yourself for the strict training.
  你要為這個嚴格的訓練做好準備。

練習時間試試看

確認訂單內容

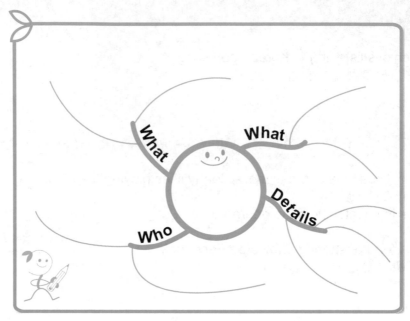

 Who are you writing to?　對象

 What is this email for?　主旨

 What will the other party do for you?　對方為你做什麼

 Details of the work / project　工作細節

練習範例分享

Dear Ms. Lee,
I'm so delighted to have such an experienced wedding planner as you to help me put together the most important event in my life, my wedding ceremony scheduled on Sun. December 19th. I enjoyed meeting with you last Friday discussing the outlines for the wedding of my dream!

主旨

對方為你做什麼

According to the contract we signed when we met, you will be preparing the following details two months ahead of the ceremony:
Compile the guest's list, and update their contact information
Order invitation cards and cake coupons
Choose the gifts for the wedding the party
Discuss the menu requirement with the party venue, or better yet, arrange a tasting dinner
Discuss the venue setup specifications with the hotel
Try out the makeup and hairstyle
Confirm the transportation arrangements
Finalize the seating plan
Please confirm the above details and I'd like to schedule further meetings for my hairdo and venue setup.
Look forward to your counseling.

工作細節

主旨

Yours truly,
Bella Whitman

李小姐您好，

很高興能請到像您這樣經驗豐富的婚禮策劃高手，為我打造我這一生最重要的場合－我的婚禮（預定在12月19日星期日舉辦）。我很開心上週五和您見面討論我夢想中的婚禮的雛型。
根據我們見面當天簽訂的合約，您會在婚禮前兩個月完成以下事項：
彙整賓客名單和更新聯絡資料
訂邀請卡及蛋糕券
選婚宴禮物
和會場討論餐宴需求，並安排婚宴菜餚試吃
和會場討論佈置細節
試化新娘妝和髮型
確認當天禮車以及交通安排
確認賓客座位
請確認以上細節，我也想跟您敲定後續和您見面的時間，以進一步討論新娘裝扮和場地佈置的時間。
期待您提供諮詢。

Bella Whitman敬上

Unit 10

廠商

情境一
詢問規格

情境二
約定交貨

情境三
詢問發票

 情境一　詢問規格

心智圖解說

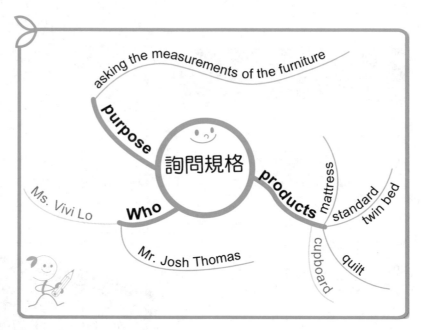

寫作技巧錦囊

 Who are you writing to?　你要寫給誰
→ Mr. Josh Thomas

 What products are you interested in purchasing?　你有興趣購買什麼產品
→ standard twin bed, mattress & quilt

 What is the purpose of this email?　這封email的目的是什麼
→ asking the measurements of the furniture

單字片語搶先看

1. **standard** *n.[C,U] adj.* 標準；規格；標準的
   - Searching luggage at airports is now standard practice.
   檢查行李已經是機場的標準執行步驟。

2. **measurements** *n.[P]* 尺寸
   - Take measurements of the room before you buy any new furniture.
   在買新家具之前，要先丈量屋子的大小。
   詞類變化：measure *vi. vt.* 量；測量

3. **dimensions** *n. [P]* 尺寸（長寬高）
   - What are the dimensions of the TV set?
   這台電視的尺寸為何？

4. **inch** *n.[C]* 英吋
   - He just bought a flat TV which is 24-inch wide.
   他剛買了一部24吋寬的電視。

5. **foot** *n.[C]* 英尺
   - This giant penguin stands almost 4 feet and 5 inches tall.
   這隻巨大的企鵝站著將近有4英尺5英吋高。

6. **wide** *adj.* 寬的 *(=offer, provide)*
   - How wide is the door? It's almost 2 feet wide.
   這扇門有多寬？約有兩英尺寬。
   詞類變化：width *n.[C,U]* 寬度

7. **length** *n.[C,U]* 長度
   - We measured the length and width of the living room.
   我們丈量客廳的長度和寬度。
   詞類變化：long *adj.* 長的

英文範例

詢問規格

To Mr. Josh Thomas, ── 對象

★ I am looking for a bed, mattress, and comforter for my

bedroom. I am very interested in the standard twin bed ── 產品

(No. TL525) and its matching mattress and quilt listed on ── 產品 產品

your online furniture catalog. But I have a few questions

regarding the measurements of the furniture. ── 主旨

I'd like to know the dimensions of the bed and mattress.

As for the comforter, I am over 5'8" inches tall. I expect

nothing smaller than a full five feet wide and 80 inches

in length.

Please provide detailed measurements about the above

items.

Thank you and I look forward to hearing from you.

Sincerely,

Bobby Lincecum

段落大意

寫信目的	開場自我介紹，點出對該公司產品有興趣，想要詢價。
請教細節	請對方提供商品的尺寸。
懇請回覆	要求對方回覆。
信尾	客套語 + 署名。

中文翻譯

Josh Thomas您好，

我正在為我的臥室尋找床組（床架，床墊和棉被）。我對你們網站型錄上的標準單人床（編號TL525）以及配套的床墊和棉被很感興趣，但我對於尺寸有些疑問。

我想要知道床架和床墊的尺寸，至於棉被的部分，我身高超過5英尺8英吋，我想要找的棉被大小不能小於5英尺寬和80英吋長。
請提供上述物件詳細的尺寸。
謝謝您，期待您的回覆。

Bobby Lincecum敬上

換個對象寫寫看

產品規格

- Please send me the product specifications of Dell Optiplex 700 tablet. I'd like to know about the size, including height, width, depth, and weight.
  請提供Dell 型號Optiplex 700平板電腦的產品說明書，我想知道尺寸相關的規格，包含高度、寬度、厚度以及重量。

產品性能

- I'd like to know about the product features of the new i-Pad. Please provide the details for its storage capacity, and features of its display, cameras, photos, and video recording. I'm curious about its operating system and system requirements.
  我想知道新i-Pad的產品性能，請提供以下細節：記憶體容量以及顯示器、照相、相片及錄影的性能，我也很好奇它的操作系統以及系統需求。

其他詢問產品規格的的句型

- Please provide the product description details of model ____.
  請提供型號 ____的產品說明細節。
- I'd like to know more about features of your digital camera model ____.
  我想要知道更多有關數位相機型號 ____的產品性能。
- We would highly appreciate it if you can forward the product description and specification of your TG LED(4W)
  若您能附上TG LED(4W)的產品說明與規格細節，我們將非常感激。
- Full / Detailed information regarding carton size and cubic capacity would be very appreciated.
  若能詳列外箱尺寸和裝櫃數量，將會讓我十分感激。

句型解說在這裡

句型1

度量單位「形容詞」用法

直述句句型：物品 + is + 數字 + 度量單位 + long / wide / deep / thick / tall / high

- The table is two meters long.
  這張桌子有兩公尺長。
- The basketball player is two meters tall.
  這位籃球選手有兩公尺高。

問句句型：How + long / wide / deep / thick / tall / high + is + 物品

- How deep is the pond?
  這個池塘有多深？
- How high is the mountain?
  這座山有多高？

特殊句型：How much do / does + S + weigh(v.) + 數字 + 度量單位

- How much does this tablet computer weigh? It weighs 1 kilogram.
  這個平板電腦有多重？一公斤重。

度量單位「形容詞」用法

直述句句型：物品 + is + 數字 + 度量單位 + in + length / width / depth / height / weight

- The pond is eighty centimeters deep.= The pond is eighty centimeters in depth.
  這個池塘有八十公分深。

問句句型：What is the + length, width, depth, height, weight + of + 物品

- How wide is the table? = What's the width of the table?
  這張桌子有多長？
- How deep is the pond? = What's the depth of the pond?
  這個池塘有多深？

練習時間試試看

詢問規格

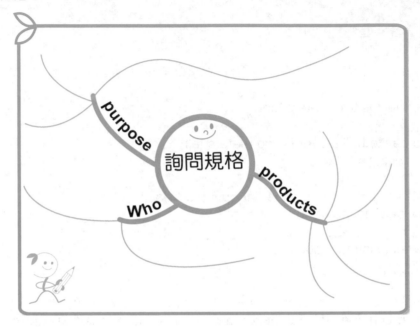

 Step 1   Who are you writing to? 你要寫給誰？

 Step 2   What products are you interested in purchasing?
你有興趣購買什麼產品？

 Step 3   What is the purpose of this email? 這封email的目的是什麼？

練習範例分享

To Mr. Richardson,

對象

★ I am looking for a refrigerator for my kitchen. I am very

interested in your award winning Domestic Refrigerator

主旨

(CR-1051) listed on your online furniture catalog. But I

產品

have a few questions regarding the measurements and

features.

I'd like to know the dimensions of the refrigerator.

Besides, can you tell me the details of the features? I'm

also wondering how many colors to chose from.

Thank you and I look forward to hearing from you.

Sincerely,

Claire Lee

Richardson先生您好，

我正在為我的廚房尋找冰箱。我對你們網站型錄上有得獎的家用冰箱（編號CR-1051）感興趣，但我對於尺寸和性能有些疑問。
我想要知道冰箱的尺寸，此外您是否能告訴我詳細的性能？我也想知道我有多少有少顏色可以選擇。
謝謝您，期待您的回覆。

Claire 李敬上

情境二　約定交貨

心智圖解說

寫作技巧錦囊

Who are you writing to?　這封信寫給誰
→ Ms. Eileen Cooper

What is the purpose of this email?　這封email的目的是什麼
→ the delivery date of the order

What did you order?　你訂了什麼
→ printers, ink cartridge, A4 paper

When did you order the goods?　你什麼時候訂的
→ October 19th

When do you want the ordered goods to be delivered?
你希望的到貨時間
→ October 25th

單字片語搶先看

1. **concerning** *adj.* 關於…… *(=about)*
   - I'm writing this email concerning the delivery date of my order.
   我寫信來詢問有關我的訂單交貨時間。

2. **laser** *n.[C]* 雷射
   - The laser eye surgery has both benefits and possible risks.
   雷射眼睛手術有其好處和可能的風險。

3. **printer** *n.[C]* 印表機
   - Most customers prefer color-laser printers to inkjet printers.
   大部分的顧客喜愛彩色雷射印表機勝過噴墨印表機。

4. **ink** *n.[U]* 墨水
   - There's no need to toss out your pen when ink runs dry. You can purchase ink to refill the pen
   當你的筆沒有墨水時不必丟掉。你可以買墨水來填充。

5. **cartridge** *n.[C]* 墨水匣；筆芯
   - Most suppliers instruct their customers to replace ink cartridges when the cartridge is still half of ink.
   大部分供應商會叫客戶在墨水匣還在半滿狀態下更換墨水匣。

6. **ream** *n.[C]* 一令 (紙張計數單位，為500或516張)
   - Our company just ordered 500 reams of A4 copy paper from the manufacturer directly.
   我們公司剛和製造商直接下單購買500令的A4影印紙。

7. **then** *adv.* 當時
   - The deadline of the report is November 10th. You need to submit your work by then.
   報告繳交時間是11月10日。你要在那之前繳交。

英文範例

約定交貨

【★可替換其他交貨時間訴求】

Dear Ms. Cooper,　　　　　　　　　　　　　　　　對象

I'm writing this email concerning the delivery time of my

order made on October 19th (Order No. 6520), which　　下單時間

includes:　　　　　　　　　　　　　　　　　　　　主旨

2 laser printers　　　　　　　　　　　　　　　　　產品

5 ink cartridge　　　　　　　　　　　　　　　　　產品

10 reams of A4 paper (white)　　　　　　　　　　　產品

★ I'd like to know how long it usually takes for the

goods to be delivered. I hope we can receive the

ordered items by October 25th. Please confirm if our

order can arrive by then.

Looking forward to having from you soon,　　　　　希望的到貨時間

Yours sincerely,

Candy Jones

段落大意

寫信目的　開場簡述訂單內容。

約定交貨時間　提出希望收到貨品的日期與時間。

懇請回覆　要求對方回覆確認可否配合。

信尾　客套語 + 署名。

中文翻譯

Cooper小姐您好,

我寫這封信是要問有關於我在10月19日所下的訂單（訂單號碼6520）的交貨時間。訂購商品包含:
2台雷射印表機
5個墨水匣
10令A4用紙（白色）
我想知道通常你們送貨要花多久時間。我希望我們可以在10月25日前收到訂購的品項。
請您確認我們的商品是否可以在那之前送達。
期待盡快收到您的回覆。

Candy Jones敬上

換個對象寫寫看

再次詢問交貨時間

The goods we ordered (No. 56250) on October 19th were supposed to arrive on October 23rd. But It's already October 25th and we still haven't received them yet. We'd like to know what caused the delay. And please notify when you will deliver the items.

我們在10月19日訂購的商品（訂單編號56250）原定應該在10月23日就送達了，但現在已經是10月25日，我們卻還沒收到。我們想了解為何送貨時間會拖延，也請你們通知何時會送貨。

希望更早交貨

We'd like to request for express delivery of our order made on October 19th(Order No. 6520). It's originally scheduled to arrive on October 25th. However, is it possible that we can receive the goods by October 23rd? Please confirm if you can make the delivery and let us know if there' s additional charge for express delivery.

我們很想請您盡快寄送我們在10月19日訂購的商品（訂單編號56250）。該訂單商品原本預定會在10月25日送達，但我們想問有可能可以在10月23日前收到這批物品嗎？請確認您們是否可以速件處理該訂單，也請讓我們知道你們是否要額外收取快遞的費用。

其他討論交貨時間的句型

Could you tell us how long it is likely to take you to deliver the goods?
可否請你們告知送貨可能要花多久時間？

We'd like to know when you can make the delivery of order No. _____.
我們想知道你們何時可以寄出訂單編號 _____ 的商品。

We would appreciate it if the goods of our order No. _____ can arrive by October 25th.
若能在10月25日前收到訂單編號 _____ 的商品，我們將十分感激。

I'd like to know if it's possible that we can receive the order No. _____ by October 25th.
我們想知道是否能在10月25日前收到訂單編號_____的貨品。

句型解說在這裡

句型1

關係代名詞which / that的用法

取代同一句子內的先行詞「事／物／動物」，可以用that取代。

- I have lost the watch. My mom bought me the watch last year.
  → I have lost the watch which / that my mom bought me last year.
  我搞丟了我媽去年買給我的手錶。
  (which指的是句子前半段提到的the watch)

取代逗點前的整個句子，不可以用that 取代，此處which是單數名詞，後面接單數動詞。

- I have lost the watch. It made Mom very angry.
  → I have lost the watch, which makes Mom very angry.
  我搞丟了手錶，這件事讓媽媽很生氣。
  (which指的是逗點前整句話I lost the watch)

句型2

How long does it take sb. to V　某人花了多少時間做……？

- How long does it take the technician to fix the car?
  技術人員花了多少時間修理這輛車？

It takes sb. ＋時間 ＋ to V　某人花了多少時間做……

- It takes the mechanic 2 hours to fix the car.
  維修人員修理這輛車要花兩小時。

練習時間試試看

約定交貨時間

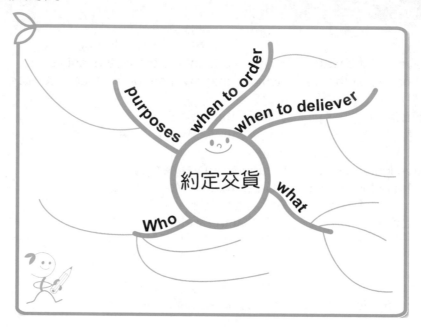

 Step 1 Who are you writing to? 這封信寫給誰

 Step 2 What is the purpose of this email? 這封email的目的是什麼

 Step 3 What did you order? 你訂了什麼

 Step 4 When did you order the goods? 你什麼時候訂的

 Step 5 When do you want the ordered goods to be delivered?
你希望的到貨時間

練習範例分享

Dear Ms. Wills,

I'm writing this email to request speed delivery of my order — 對象 / 主旨

made on November 11th (Order No. 6520). — 下單時間

The items include:

2 x P-48C Cross Cut Shredder (Black)

200 x Correction Tape (Pack of 2) — 下單內容

100 x Rapid Correction Fluid — 下單內容

50 x Epson A4 Paper (White, 500 Sheets) — 下單內容

I know it usually takes 5 working days to make a — 下單內容

delivery. However, is there any possibility that you can

speed deliver the above items by November 14th? We — 希望到貨時間

would much appreciate it if you can help make the

speed delivery.

Looking forward to your confirmation,

Yours Sincerely,

Belly Silverstone

Wills小姐您好，

我寫這封信是要問我在11月11日所下的訂單（訂單號碼6520）可否以速件出貨。
訂購商品包含：
2台P-48C機型碎紙機（黑色）
200套修正帶（一套包含兩個）
100個修正液
50包Epson A4紙（白色，每包500張）
我知道通常你們送貨要花5個工作天。但你們是否有可能盡速出貨，在11月14日前送達該批訂單？若能盡速出貨，我們會很感激。
期待盡快收到您的回覆確認。

Belly Silverstone敬上

情境三 詢問發票

心智圖解說

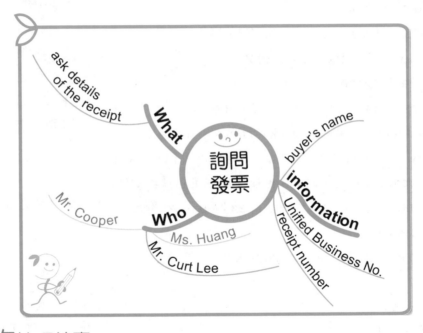

寫作技巧錦囊

 Step 1 Who are you writing to? 你要寫給誰
→ Mr. Curt Lee

 Step 2 What is the purpose of this email? 這封email的目的是什麼
→ asking details of the receipt

 Step 3 the information shown on the receipt 發票上的資訊
→ receipt number, buyer's name, Unified Business No.

單字片語搶先看

1. **money order** 匯票
   - I'm about to cash the money order at the bank.
   我等一下要去銀行將匯票兌現。

2. **receipt** *n.[C]* 收據
   - Fill out the information on the sales receipt, tear off one copy for your customer and keep a copy for your business records.
   填好收據後，撕下收執聯給客戶，商家自己保留存根聯記帳用。
   詞類變化：receive *vi. vt.* 收到

3. **package** *n.[C]* 包裹
   - My package arrived safely without any cracks the day after I paid it.
   我的包裹在我付款一天後就送達了，完好無缺損。

4. **include** *vt.* 包含
   - Does the bill include tax and service charge?
   這筆帳單款項含稅以及服務費嗎？

5. **name / title of the address** 收據抬頭
   - I'd like to include the name of the address on my receipt, in order to be reimbursed for business expenses.
   我想要收據上註明抬頭，以便回公司報公帳。

6. **Business Registration Number** 營業註冊登記編號
   - The public can enquire the business registration number of a business.
   一般大眾可以查詢一家企業的營業登記證。

7. **Unified Business Number** 統一編號 (=Business Registration Code / Company Tax ID / Unified Business Identifier (UBI) number)
   - You need to fill in Business License application to obtain the Unified Business Number for your company.
   你要填寫營利事業登記申請，以替你的公司取得統一編號。

英文範例

詢問發票

Dear Mr. Lee,
— 對象

Thank you so much for shopping (Order No. 84512)

through our website. We received your payment of

NT$12,500 via money order on November 12th. The

goods will be shipped tomorrow along with the receipt,

and the package is supposed to be delivered by

November 17th.
— 發票資訊

We have one question regarding the receipt. Would

you like to include the name / title of the addressee

and Business Registration Code or Unified Business

Number?
— 主旨

Look forward to your reply regarding the receipt today.

Sincerely,

Andria Tseng

段落大意

寫信目的	開場說明訂單已收到貨款和出貨事宜。
發票細節	請教對方發票上是否要附上抬頭或統編。
懇請回覆	要求對方回覆確認。
信尾	客套語 ＋ 署名。

中文翻譯

李先生您好，

謝謝您透過我們網站購物（訂單編號84512）。我們已經在11月12日收到貨款12500元幣的匯票。商品明天會連同發票一起出貨，包裹將於11月17日前送達。

我們有個關於發票的疑問。您希望我們在發票上註明收據抬頭以及營業登記號碼或統一編號嗎？

期待您能今天回覆。

Andria 曾 敬上

單據說明看這裡

如何填寫請款單

Best Company

Bill to : C1007
① ABC Company
123 Big Forest Valley
Ottawa, On Z12345
Canada

DATE: November 30, 2012
INVOICE# INV1000
② Ship to :
SH Name 1
SH Address 1
SH CityState 1 SHZ12345
USA

③ P.O. #	④ Sales Rep. Name	⑤ Ship Date	⑥ Ship Via	⑦ Terms	Due Date
O200612005	sales	11/30/2012	UPS	Net 7 ⑧	

⑨ Product ID	⑩ Description	⑪ Quantity	⑫ Unit Price	⑬ Line Total
P1003	Motorola E815	10	420.00	4,200.00
P1000	Nokia 3220	12	199.99	2,399.88
P1004	Non-taxable item	5	200.00	1,000.00
P1002	It is a service	3.2	255.52	817.66
P1006	Motorola V3 Razr Black	10	500.00	5,000.00

Notes:

⑭ SUBTOTAL		13,417.54
⑮ PST	6.50%	807.14
⑯ GST	3.20%	397.36
⑰ SHIPPING & HANDING		-
TOTAL		14,622.04
PAID		-
⑱ TOTAL DUE		14,622.04

如何填寫發票

RECEIPT

Date ____ / ____ / ____   Number _____

Received from _____ $ _____

_____ Dollars

For Payment of _____

From _____ To _____

⑲ Amount Due		
⑳ Amt Paid		
㉑ Balance		

☐ Cash
☐ Check ㉒   ㉓ Check No. _____
☐ Money Order   Money Order No. _____
☐ Credit Card

Memo _____   By _____

詞彙說明

1. 發票寄送地址
2. 收貨地址
3. 訂單編號
4. 銷售員姓名
5. 出貨時間
6. 送貨方式
7. 付款方式
8. 請在請款單開立後7天內付款
9. 商品代號
10. 品項說明
11. 數量
12. 商品單價
13. 單品項總金額
14. 小計
15. 地方省府課徵的消費稅
16. 消費與服務稅
17. 運費和服務費
18. 請款總金額
19. 應繳金額
20. 已繳金額
21. 餘額（尚須繳納的金額）
22. 支票
23. 匯票

句型解說在這裡

句型1

by + V-ing 藉由做……
by means of + N 藉由……方式
with + N

- I apologized to her by sending a text message.
  我用傳簡訊的方式向她道歉。
- I escaped by means of a secret tunnel.
  我從一個秘密通道逃走了。
- Chop the onions with a sharp knife.
  用這把鋒利的刀切洋蔥。

be supposed to V 應該會

- This parcel is supposed to arrive by Friday.
  這包裹應該在週五前送達。

搭配被動語態：be supposed to be p.p.

- This parcel is supposed to be shipped by Friday.
  這包裹應該在週五前被寄達。

不定詞搭配被動語態：to be p.p.

- He doesn't want to be eliminated from the competition.
  他不想從比賽中被淘汰。
- The scandal of this government official has to be revealed to the public.
  這名官員的醜聞必須被揭發。

練習時間試試看

詢問發票

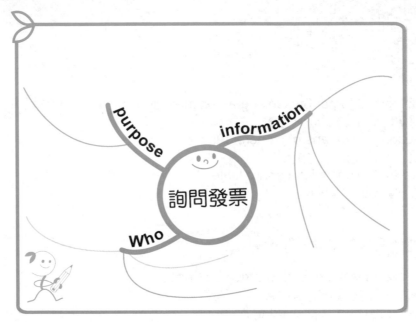

 Step 1　Who are you writing to?　你要寫給誰

 Step 2　What is the purpose of this email?　這封email的目的是什麼

 Step 3　the information shown on the receipt　發票上的資訊

練習範例分享

Dear Ms. Lin,

對象

Thank you so much for purchasing cosmetics and skin

care products (Order No. 84512) through Beauty Buy.

com. We received your payment of NT$8990 via ATM on

Feb 15th. The goods will be shipped tomorrow along with

the receipt, and the package is supposed to arrive by

Feb 20th.

發票資訊

As for the receipt, would you like the name / title of the

addressee and Unified Business Number to be shown

on the receipt?

主旨

Your prompt reply would be much appreciated.

Sincerely,

Andy Chang

林小姐您好，

謝謝您透過Beauty Buy.com網站購買化妝品和保養品（訂單編號84512）我們已經在2月15日收到您ATM轉帳貨款8990台幣。商品明天會連同發票一起出貨，您應該會在2月20日前收到包裹。

至於發票，您希望我們在發票上註明收據抬頭以及統一編號嗎？

您若能盡速回覆，我們將十分感激。

Andy 張 敬上

Unit 11

客服

情境一
會立即改善

情境二
通知取貨

情境三
回覆使用問題

情境一　會立即改善

心智圖解說

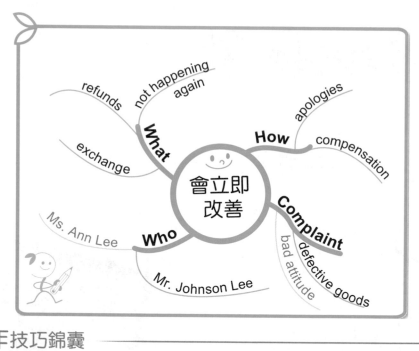

寫作技巧錦囊

Step 1
Who are you writing to?　你要寫給誰？
→ Mr. Johnson Lee

Step 2
What did the customer **complain** about?　客戶抱怨什麼？
→ defective goods

Step 3
How do you respond to the complaint?　你如何回應客訴？
→ apologies, compensation

Step 4
What will you deal with the problem?　你會如何處理這個問題？
→ refunds, exchange, not happening again

單字片語搶先看

1. shipment *n.[C,U]* 裝運；裝載的貨物
   ☞ We received the shipment of books this Friday。
   我們在本週五收到送來的書。

2. error *n.[C,U]* 錯誤；犯錯誤
   ☞ This error in transaction has caused him millions of dollars.
   交易過程的錯誤讓他損失好幾百萬美金。

3. in the meantime 同時 *(= meanwhile)*
   ☞ The police are tracking down the suspect. In the meantime, they have talked to all the witnesses.
   警方正在追蹤這個嫌疑犯。在此同時，他們也已經約談了所有證人。

4. merchandise *n.[U]* 商品
   ☞ This store is filled with merchandise exported from Korea.
   這間店到處都是南韓進口的商品。

5. assure *vt.* 向……保證
   ☞ We assure you that we will take the responsibility and compensate your loss.
   我們向您保證我們會負起責任並賠償您的損失。

6. maintain *vt.* 維持 (= keep)
   ☞ A good restaurant will maintain consistent good quality in both services and cuisine.
   一間好的餐廳會維持服務和菜餚的一貫高品質。

7. prevent…from V-ing 預防……的發生
   ☞ You should drive carefully to prevent any accident from happening.
   你要小心開車，預防車禍的發生。

英文範例

【★可替換其他因應對策】

對象：客戶

Dear Mr. Lee,　　　　　　　　　　　　　　　　　　● 對象

We have received your email on June 23rd, claiming that you have found defects in the goods of our shipment.　　● 抱怨事項

★ We were extremely sorry for the error and we are dealing with the problem at this very moment.　　● 如何回應

We will certainly help with returns of the goods. We will send someone today to collect the entire shipment.　　● 未來處理方式

In the meantime we have already sent another shipment of perfect merchandise to you, which should arrive no later than tomorrow evening.　　● 如何回應

Please accept our sincere apologies for any inconvenience this may have caused. We assure you that we will take measures to maintain good quality to prevent any similar problems from happening again.

　　　　　　　　　　　　　　　　　　　　● 未來處理方式

Sincerely yours,

Jack Middleson

段落大意

寫信目的　　開場簡述訂單內容。

收到客戶反應　開場說明已收到顧客反映的問題，再陳述一次問題細節。

正在積極處理中　具體說明處理的方式和進度等細節。

懇請等候　　懇請對方給你時間靜候處理結果。

信尾　　客套語 + 署名。

中文翻譯

李先生您好，

我們已收到您在6月23日的郵件，信中您提到在給您的貨物中有貨品出現瑕疵。我們對此失誤萬感抱歉，此刻正積極處理中。
我們當然會協助退貨。今天我們就會派人取回整批貨物。

在此同時，我們也已經重新出貨，寄出完好無缺的貨品給您，應該明天傍晚前就會送達。

對任何可能造成您的不便，請接受我們誠摯的歉意。我們向您保證一定會採取措施維持好的品質，以確保類似問題不會再發生。

Jack Middleson 敬上

換個對象寫寫看

交貨時間延遲

- Please accept our apologies for the failure to deliver your ordered goods at the scheduled time in accordance with the contract we have signed. We were unable to fill all orders due to the excessive demand during the high season in the past two weeks. We have already sent the goods to you this morning. We'd like to inform you that we will still compensate you for your loss owing to the unintended violation of the contract terms.

  我們很抱歉沒有按照合約上的預定時間寄出您訂購的貨品。因為前兩個禮拜旺季的需求太多，無法消化所有訂單。我們已經在今早送出貨品。我們要通知您因為意外違反合約，我們仍會賠償您的損失。

運送過程中貨品受損

- We were extremely sorry to learn that your ordered goods were damaged on arrival. If we were to be responsible for the matter, we would replace these damaged items. However, as we confirmed with our warehouse staff, all the goods were carefully and perfectly packed and sent out in good condition. We have the clean B / L to prove this, and we have sent you a copy for your reference. It was evident that the damaged was caused due to careless handling in the shipping process. Please wait as we are currently negotiating with the shipping company as to how to settle the matter. We'll get back to you a.s.a.p.

  我們很抱歉得知您所訂購的商品在抵達時受損。若我們要為此事負責，定當為您換貨。但我們和倉管人員確認過了，所有的貨物在出貨時，都是完好無缺，且都被仔細打包好才出貨。我們有提單可以證明，且也已經寄了一份副本給您參考。很明顯損害是在貨運過程中粗心所致。我們正在和貨運公司交涉如何處理此事，我們會儘快回覆給您。

其他回應顧客抱怨的萬用句型

- We were terribly sorry for damaging the goods you ordered.
  對於不小心毀損您的商品我們深感抱歉。
- We will immediately send the rest of your ordered goods.
  我們會立刻寄送您訂單中其他的部分。

句型解說在這裡

句型1

S + 助動詞 (can / should / may / must) + VR

- This shipment you ordered should arrive no later than tomorrow evening.
  您訂購的貨物應該會在明天傍晚前送達。

延伸觀念

ought to + VR = should + VR　應該

- You ought to apologize to him. = You should apologize to him.
  他應該向他道歉。

be able to + VR = can + VR　有能力會做

- He is able to prepare dinner for 300 people. = He can prepare dinner for 300 people.
  他能為300人準備晚餐

have to + VR = need to + VR = must + VR　必須去做

- He has to / needs to finish the report tonight. = He must finish the report tonight.
  他必須今晚完成報告。

S + 助動詞 (can / should / may / must) + have + p.p.　對過去事件的推測

should + have + p.p.　本來應該要做……(但結果沒做)

- You should have told me the truth. Now I can't help you.
  你早該跟我說實話的，現在我沒法幫你了。

must + have p.p.　一定已經……了 (對過去事件十分有把握的肯定猜測)

- The ground is wet. It must have rained earlier this afternoon.
  地板是濕的，稍早一定下過雨。

might / may + have p.p.　應該已經……了(對過去事件沒有把握的猜測)

He hasn't come yet. He may have been caught in the traffic jam.
  他還沒到。他現在可能塞在車陣裡。

can't + have p.p.　一定不可能已經……了(對過去事件很有把握的否定猜測)

- He can't have gone to bed. The lights are still on in his room.
  他不可能去睡了。他房間燈還亮著。

練習時間試試看

會立即改善

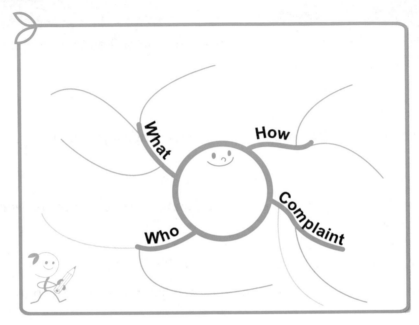

 Who are you writing to?　對象

 What did the customer **complain** about?　抱怨事項

 How do you respond to the complaint?　如何回應

 What will you deal with the problem?　未來處理方式

練習範例分享

Dear Ms. Chen,

→ 對象

We were extremely sorry to know that you purchased 4

Mascaras in your order No. 2512 but only received 2 in

our shipment.

→ 抱怨事項
→ 未來處理方式

Please accept our sincere apologies for the errors

in the shipment. We will deliver the rest of the items

immediately, which will arrive no later than tomorrow

afternoon. Besides, for compensation, we'll enclose a

free sample for the latest BB cream in this shipment.

→ 如何回應

We hope you can forgive us for this unintentional

mistake and continue to purchase goods from us.

→ 未來處理方式

Sincerely yours,

Jason Milton

陳小姐您好,

很抱歉得知在您的訂單號碼2512中,您原本訂購了4支睫毛膏,但實際收貨時只收到2支。

針對出貨過程的疏失,請接受我們誠摯的歉意。我們會立刻寄送短缺的貨品,貨物會在明天下午前送達。此外,為了彌補您,我們會附上一罐最新出的BB霜試用品。希望您能原諒我們無意的疏失,並持續向我們訂購產品。

Jason Milton敬上

情境二　通知取貨

心智圖解說

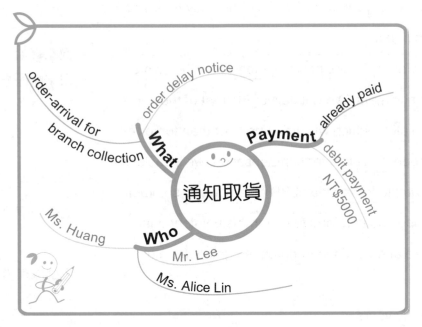

寫作技巧錦囊

 Who are you writing to?　對象
→ Ms. Alice Lin

 What is this email for?　主旨
→ order-arrival for branch collection

 Payment status　付款狀態
→ already paid

單字片語搶先看

1. **dispatch** *vt.* 寄送 *(= send)*
   - We'll email you when your order is dispatched and also when it's ready to collect.
   當您的訂購商品已經被寄出以及可以取貨時，我們會以電郵通知您。

2. **branch** *n. [C]* 門市；分店；分公司
   - We have got the item you ordered from one of our branches.
   我們已經從門市之一調貨取得您訂購的商品。

3. **collect** *vi. vt.* 堆積；收集
   - Please feel free to collect your order at your nominated branch at your convenience.
   歡迎在您有空時到您指定的門市取貨。

4. **opening hours** 營業時間
   - The opening hours of our campus branch are Monday - Friday: 09:00 - 18:00.
   我們的學校門市部的營業時間是週一到週五早上九點到晚上六點。

5. **alteration** *n.[C]* 修改
   - This tailor specializes in alterations, dressmaking and tailoring, including wedding parties and prom dresses.
   這位裁縫師專精服裝修改，訂製洋裝或量身訂做衣服，包含製作婚宴派對或畢業舞會用的洋裝。
   詞類變化：alter *vi. vt.*

6. **patronage** *n.[U]* 光顧
   - Thank you for your past and continued patronage to our salon.
   謝謝您過去和現在持續到我們美髮沙龍光顧。

7. **growth** *n.[U]* 成長
   - Achieve sustained profitable growth by putting your customers at the heart of your strategy.
   要達到穩健獲利的成長，要靠以客為尊的策略。
   詞類變化：grow *vi. vt.* 成長；使生長

英文範例

通知取貨　　　　　　　　　　　【★可替換其他取貨提醒】

Dear Ms. Lin,　　　　　　　　　　　　　　　　　→ 對象

We're please to inform you that the following items

of your order No. 5212 have been dispatched to your

chosen branch.　　　　　　　　　　　　　　　→ 主旨

1 x wool Military Coat (size 10)

2 x washed T-shirt with pockets (beige, size 8)

1 x camouflage print trousers (size 8)

★ You are welcome to collect your order during our

opening hours 11:00 am ~8:00 p.m. Tuesday through

Sunday. You have paid the full amount of NT$ 8,900

on June 23rd and there are no extra charges for the　→ 對象

alteration to the length of the trousers.

　　　　　　　　　　　　　　　　　　　　→ 如何回應

Your continued patronage and suggestions are a vital

part of our growth. And for that, we are most grateful.

Thanks again! We look forward to serving you for many

years to come.

Yours Sincerely,

Susan Norms

段落大意

商品已抵達	開場感謝對方購買某件商品,商品已抵達。
取貨細節	說明取貨及付款細節。
懇請回覆	要求對方回覆確認,希望對方儘早來取貨。
信尾	客套語 + 署名。

中文翻譯

林小姐您好,

您日前的訂單編號5212的商品已經被送至您指定的門市了。商品明細如下:

1 X 羊毛海軍風外套 (尺碼10號)
2 X 水洗T恤(附口袋) (肉色,尺碼8號)
1 X 迷彩印花褲子 (尺碼8號)

歡迎您在門市營業時間(早上11點到晚上8點,週二到週日)到店取貨。您已經在6月23日付清所有款項,新台幣8,900元。您訂購的褲子長度修改不另外收費。

您持續的光顧和給我們的建議一直是我們成長的重要動力,讓我們十分感激。

再次謝謝您。希望未來能為您服務長長久久。

Susan Norms敬上

換個對象寫寫看

【★可替換其他取貨提醒】

只有付訂金，必須要付清尾款

☞ You're welcome to visit the above retail branch to collect the goods. Please be notified that the total amount of the order is NT$8,999. You have paid NT$2,000. Please remit the debit payment of NT$6,999 when you collect the items.

歡迎您到以上門市取貨。提醒您訂購品項的總金額是新台幣8,999元。您已經先付了2,000元，尚餘6,999元，請在取貨時結清。

部分貨品已經沒有現貨或庫存

☞ The washed T-shirts with pockets and camouflage print trousers you ordered have just arrived. As for the wool Military Coat (size 10), we're sorry it's out of stock due to high demand for this size. But we do have the same coat coming in other sizes for you choose from. If the other sizes don't fit, we'll return your prepaid amount NT$ 3,999 for the coat.

您訂購的水洗T恤（附口袋）以及迷彩印花褲已經到貨了。至於羊毛軍裝風大衣（尺碼10號），很抱歉已經沒有庫存，因為這個尺碼很搶手。但我們有同款大衣的其他尺碼可供您挑選。若您試穿後覺得不合身，我們就會退還該大衣您預先付清的費用台幣3,999元。

其他提醒取貨或沒有貨品的常用句型

☞ Thank you for considering our company. This email notification is to inform you that the order you placed last week has just hit the shelves. Please feel free to collect your merchandise at your convenience.

謝謝您考慮本公司。這封信是要提醒您：您上週所下的訂單貨品已經抵達。歡迎您在有空時來取貨。

☞ The items you requested were out of stock at the time you placed the order. But we are very glad to inform you that we have got them sent from one of other branches. You're very welcome to stop by and collect your order.

您所訂購的品項在您下訂當時正缺貨。但我們很開心要通知您我們已經從其他門市調貨成功了。歡迎您有空順道來取貨。

句型解說在這裡

句型1

p.p.當形容詞表示「被動」

- Thank you for your continued patronage.
  謝謝您持續的光顧。
- You can collect your ordered items at your chosen branch.
  你可以在你指定的門市拿你訂的商品。

延伸觀念

- The stolen wallet was sent to Lost and Found.
  被偷的錢包被送到失物招領處。

p.p.當形容詞表示「已經」

- The farmer picked up the fallen fruit, which was rotten to the core.
  農夫撿起落果，都腐爛了。

p.p.當形容詞情緒動詞p.p.表示「感到」，形容人

- The farmer was very frustrated and depressed.
  該名農夫覺得很沮喪和憂鬱。

句型2

for many years to come　在接下好幾年

- We look forward to serving you for many years to come.
  我們希望接下好幾年都可以繼續為您提供服務。

延伸句型

n + to V　用「不定詞to V」修飾名詞：還有名詞要去做⋯⋯

- We still have a long way to go before there is equal opportunity for all.
  在人人機會真正平等之前，我們還有很長一段路要走。
- He has nothing to do tonight.
  他今晚沒事做。
- He has few friends to play with.
  他幾乎沒有朋友可以陪他玩。

練習時間試試看

通知取貨

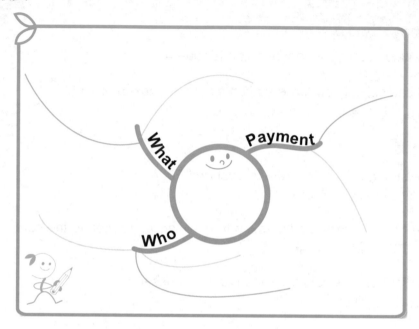

 Who are you writing to? 對象

 What is this email for? 主旨

 Payment status 付款狀態

練習範例分享

Dear Ms. Hsu,

對象

Thank you for placing an order at Mustbuy.com. We are pleased to inform you the following items you ordered on June 24th (Order No. 5212) have arrived in the store:

主旨

1 x High Rise Skinny Jeans (24 W)
2 x Boot Cut Jeans (23 W)
1 x Mid Rise Straight Fit Jeans (23 W)
1 x Low Rise Pipe Jeans (24W)

You are welcome to collect your order during our opening hours Mon-Sun,1:00 pm ~10:00 p.m. The amount of the items is NT$12,900. We also charge alterations fee NT$500 for the low rise pipe jeans, so the total amount is NT$13,400. You have made part a payment of NT$ 5,000 on June 22nd. Therefore it leaves the debit payment NT$8,400 and please remit the payment when you collect the items.

主旨

如何回應

Thanks again! We look forward to serving you soon.
Very respectfully yours,

Cassie Chu

許小姐您好,

謝謝您在Mustbuy.com上訂購產品。我們很高興通知您在6月24日下訂(編號5212)的商品已經抵達門市了。商品明細如下:
1 X 高腰顯瘦牛仔褲 (24腰)
2 X 小喇叭牛仔褲 (23腰)
1 X 中腰直筒緊身牛仔褲 (23腰)
1 X 低腰煙管褲 (24腰)
歡迎您在門市營業時間(下午1點到晚上10點,週一到週日)到店取貨。商品金額小計12,900台幣。還要收取低腰煙管褲的修改費500元,總金額共134,000台幣。您已經在6月22日先付了新台幣5,000元。因此還有尾款8,400台幣,等取貨時付清。
再次謝謝您。希望能盡快為您服務。

Cassie 朱敬上

情境三　回覆使用問題

心智圖解說

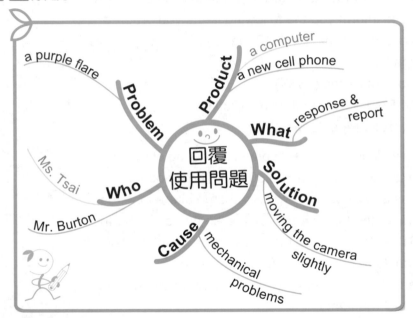

a purple flare

a computer

a new cell phone

Problem

Product

response & report

What

回覆使用問題

Solution

Ms. Tsai

Who

Mr. Burton

Cause

mechanical problems

moving the camera slightly

寫作技巧錦囊

Step 1 Who are you writing to?　對象
→ Mr. Burton

Step 2 What is this email for?　主旨
→ response & report

Step 3 What product did the consumer purchase?　產品
→ a new cell phone

Step 4 What is the problem that the customer pointed out?　問題
→ a purple flare

Step 5 Cause of the problem　成因
→ mechanical problem

Step 6 Solution to the issue　解決方法
→ Moving the camera slightly

單字片語搶先看

1. **point out** 指出
   - The analyst pointed out the country is currently suffering from economic recession.
   這位分析家指出這個國家正遭受經濟衰退之苦。

2. **issue** *n.[C]* 議題
   - Abortion is a highly controversial and widely-discussed issue.
   墮胎是個高度爭議且廣泛被討論的議題。

3. **generation** *n. [C]* 世代
   - This company is going to launch their latest generation of smartphone
   這間公司正準備要推出最新一代的智慧型手機。

4. **source** *n.[C]* 來源
   - The journalist refused to reveal his source of information.
   這位記者拒絕透露他的消息來源。

5. **sensor** *n.[C]* 感應裝置；（相機）感光元件
   - The sensor, which is the heart of a digital camera, records an image when you take a picture.
   相機的感光元件是相機的心臟，在你拍照時紀錄影像。

6. **eliminate** *vt.* 清除，刪去 *(= erase, remove)*
   - You can easily eliminate the background from a digital photo by using this image-editing program.
   你可以使用這個影像編輯軟體輕鬆將你的數位照片去背。

7. **effect** *n.[C]* 影響；現象 *(=influence)*
   - Global warming has a great effect on world climate.
   全球暖化對於全球氣候有巨大的影響。

英文範例

回覆使用問題

【★可替換其他問題與回應】

Dear Mr. Burton,　　　　　　　　　　　　　　　　　　　• 對象

We have acknowledged receiving your email last Sunday

Sept. 14th. You pointed out that ★a purple flare appeared　• 主旨

on pictures taken with the camera of your new In-Phone　• 產品

whenever it was pointed toward a bright light. Here is our　• 問題

response to the issue.　　　　　　　　　　　　　　　　　　• 問題

Most small cameras, including those in every generation

of In-Phone, may exhibit some form of flare at the edge

of the frame when capturing an image with out-of-scene

light sources. This can happen when a light source is

positioned at an angle (usually just outside the field of

view) so that it causes a reflection off the surfaces inside

the camera module and onto the camera sensor.　　　　　• 成因

Moving the camera slightly to change the position at which

the bright light is entering the lens, or shielding the lens

with your hand, should minimize or eliminate the effect.　• 解決方法

Thank you for your support to our products and we hope

you find the above suggestions helpful. Please let us

know if you have further questions or feedback.

Yours sincerely,

Frank Darabont

段落大意

感謝指教　開場感謝對方提出使用後發現的問題。

澄清與提出解決方案　顧客提出的問題不是瑕疵，而是普遍現象，可以用特定操作技巧避免。

懇請回覆　先委婉要求對方使用以上方式排除故障，若有問題再回報。

信尾　客套語 + 署名。

中文翻譯

Burton先生您好，

我們已經收到您上週日9月14日寄來的電子郵件。信中您提到每當您使用最新的In-Phone面光拍照時，會有紫色眩光出現在照片上。以下是我們對於此問題的回應。

大部分的小型照相機，包含每一代的In-Phone，都可能在螢幕外有光源的情況下，在捕捉畫面時呈現出鏡頭邊緣的光暈。這可能會發生在光源以某種角度投射（通常是光線剛好投射到鏡頭邊緣外時發生）導致在鏡頭零組件表面反射的光線被感光元件接收。照相時將角度予以調整讓光線進入鏡頭內，或用手擋在鏡頭前阻隔光線，可以大大降低甚至排除眩光的影響。

謝謝您對敝公司產品的支持，希望以上的建議能對您有所幫助。有任何進一步的疑問或回饋，歡迎與我們聯繫。

Frank Darabont 敬上

換個對象寫寫看

【★可替換其他問題與回應】

重大產品瑕疵

☞ We have acknowledged your complaints about our new maps app. We are extremely sorry for the frustration this has caused our customers and we are doing everything we can to make the system better. While we're improving system, you can try alternatives by downloading map apps from our application website.

我們已經接獲您對於我們新的地圖應用程式的抱怨。我們對於這可能造成消費者的困擾萬分抱歉，目前正盡一切全力讓這套程式變的更好。在我們改善程式的同時，您可以嘗試替代方案，例如到我們的應用程式網站下載最新的地圖搜尋應用程式。

操作不當造成的問題

☞ We have received your complaint about being unable to connect to a wireless network when using our WEP Encryption system on your tablet computer. We'd like to clarify that there is no defect in our software. The network connection failure is due to the automatic filtering in your operating system. Please follow the steps / instructions below in the order presented to resolve the issue.

我們接到您的抱怨，當您使用平板電腦操作我們WEP電腦加密程式時，就無法無線上網。我們想向您澄清我們的軟體並無瑕疵。您所遇到的無法上網的問題，主要是您電腦作業系統的自動過濾排除設定所導致。請遵照以下的步驟或操作說明，按照我們呈現的步驟，解決這個問題。

其他遇到客戶反應使用問題的回應句型

☞ We regret that our products / services have failed to live up to your expectations.
對於產品沒有達到您的期望，我們深表歉意。

☞ Thank you for your courteous comments on how to improve our products. We'll do our best to improve the quality in all our products to live up to the highest standards.
謝謝您指出我們產品可以改進的意見。我們會盡全力提升所有本公司的產品品質，以期達到最高標準。

句型解說在這裡

句型1

whenever + 句子 = every time when + 句子　　每當

- He screams whenever he sees a cockroach.
  每當他看到蟑螂他就會尖叫。
  = He screams every time when he sees a cockroach.
  每次一當他看到蟑螂他就會尖叫。
  = He screams as soon as he sees a cockroach.
  他一看到蟑螂就尖叫。
  = He never sees a cockroach without screaming.
  他沒有看到蟑螂不尖叫的時候。

延伸觀念

其他類似連接詞

whoever = anyone who = no matter who　　任何……的人

- Whoever spreads the rumor in the office will be fired.
  任何在辦公室散播謠言的人都會被開除。

wherever = anywhere = no matter where　　任何……的地方

- Wherever the singer goes, the paparazzi follows.
  任何這位歌手去的地方，狗仔都會跟著。

whatever = no matter what　　任何……的事

- Whatever you do, be cautious.
  不管你做什麼事，都請注意。

when + 句子 / 分詞　　　當……時

when 當連接詞：後面接完整句子
- He refused to make any comments when he was interviewed.
  他被訪問時，拒絕給予任何評論。

whatever = no matter what

when 後面的的子句若主詞和主要子句一致，則可刪去主詞，主要動詞改成分詞
(主動語態動詞改成V-ing，被動語態保留p.p.)
- He refused to make any comments when he was interviewed.
  = He refused to make any comments when being interviewed.
  （將he刪去，be動詞was改成being）
  = He refused to make any comments when interviewed.
  （將he刪去，被動語態只留interviewed）

練習時間試試看

回覆使用問題

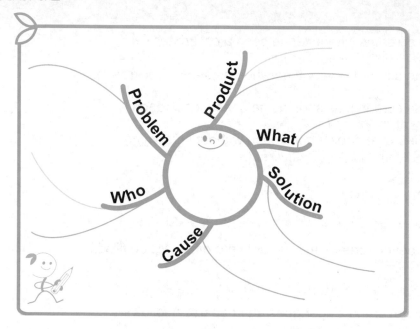

 Who are you writing to?　對象

 What is this email for?　主旨

 What **product** did the consumer purchase?　產品

 What is the **problem** that the customer pointed out?　問題

 Cause of the problem　成因

 Solution to the issue　解決方法

練習範例分享

Dear Mr. Chien,　　　　　　　　　　　　　　　　　　對象

We have acknowledged receipt of your complain about

overheating and battery drain problem in your new cell　問題

phone. Please follow the following advice to resolve

your problem easily.　　　　　　　　　　　　　　　產品

We have found that most similar problems in the same

model resulted from the slight mis-placement of the

battery. We recommend that you bring your phone to

any of our branches. Our assistant can offer to remove　成因

the battery for free and re-seat the same battery. Turn

on the phone again after a minute or so and you'll

find the battery completely cool down and you will be

pleased to find the battery can last more than a day

between charges.

Hope the above suggestions can be of help. Please　　解決方法

feel free to contact me for further questions regarding

this problem.

　　　　　　　　　　　　　　　　　　　　　　　主旨

Yours sincerely,

Kurt Goldman

簡先生您好，

我們已經收到您對您新手機容易過熱和電力很快用完的抱怨。請根據以下的建議輕鬆解決問題。

我們發現大多數發生在同款手機的類似問題都是起因於電池位置的些微誤差。我們建議您持手機到任何我們的門市。我們的店面助理人員可以免費協助取出電池，重新置入。約一分鐘後重新開機，您就會發現電池很快就降溫，也會很開心發現電池充電後可以維持超過一天。

希望以上的建議能對您有所幫助。有任何進一步的疑問或回饋，歡迎與我聯繫。

Kurt Goldman敬上

Unit 12

公關

情境一
發佈活動訊息

情境二
舉辦餐會

情境三
填寫回函

情境一　發佈活動訊息

心智圖解說

寫作技巧錦囊

Who are you writing to?　對象
→ Mr. Johnson Lee

What is this email for?　主旨
→ event announcement

What is the event?　活動
→ regular sale

What **kind** of store is having the sale?　出售商品
→ furniture

Information of the event　資訊
→ address, date

單字片語搶先看

1. **yearend clearance sale** 年終清倉大拍賣
   - Customers are long awaiting the yearend clearance sale for deeply-discounted items.
   顧客都在等年終清倉大拍賣，為了大打折扣的商品。

2. **showroom** *n.[C]* 展示間；展場；陳列室
   - The showroom presents the microphones in different recording situations.
   陳列室中展示針對不同收音情境設計的麥克風。

3. **furniture** *Plural n.* 家具
   - This sofa is the most expensive piece of furniture in our house.
   這件沙發是我們家裡最貴的家具。

4. **deal** *n.[C]* 交易
   - You can get the best deal at our anniversary sale.
   您可以在我們週年慶上獲得最超值划算的交易。

5. **household** *adj.* 家庭的
   - There are lots of household appliances to choose from at this electronic store.
   在這間電器行裡有很多家電用品可以選購。

6. **off adv.** 折扣
   - Everything is at least 30% off at this summer sale.
   在夏日特賣會中，所有商品至少下殺30% (7折)。

7. **inventory** *n.[C,U]* 財產目錄；庫存清單
   - The retailer reduces its inventory by having a big sale.
   這間零售商以大拍賣出清他的庫存。

英文範例

發佈活動訊息 　　　　　　　　　　　【★可加入其他活動訊息】

Dear Mr. Lee, ──────────────────▶ 對象

Great Furnishings is proud to announce the beginning

of our yearend furniture clearance sale! ──────▶ 活動
　　　　　　　　　　　　　　　　　　　　　　主旨

From November 1st to 14th 2013, everything in our

showroom will be marked down at least 50%! Nowhere

else in town will you find better deals on the greatest ──▶ 資訊

chairs, sofas, closets, and other household furnishings. ──▶ 出售商品

On the last day of the sale, receive an additional 10%

off everything in our store. ★ Our entire inventory

must go! Come visit us at 352 Pine Road, Da-An ──────▶ 資訊

District, Taipei City, and pick up some great furniture at

unbeatable prices! ──────────────────▶ 資訊

Sincerely,

Great Furnishings

段落大意

寫信目的 開場宣布活動主旨。

活動細節 具體說明時間地點和相關細節。

懇請光臨 懇請對方蒞臨參與。

信尾 客套語 + 署名。

中文翻譯

李先生您好：

Great家具家飾店很驕傲宣布年終清倉大拍賣要開始囉！

從2013年11月1日到14日，展示間的所有家具起標價至少下殺5折。
您不可能在城內其他地方找到更好的價格，購買品質最棒的椅子、沙發、衣櫥和其他居家家飾用品。
活動最後一天，所有家具更將再折價10%。

我們要清空所有現貨。快來台北市大安區松樹路352號，以無可比擬的超低價購買最棒的家具。

Great家具家飾店敬上

換個對象寫寫看

促銷方案

◉ Come visit us on November 14th for a special end-of-sale barbeque and live concert in the evening. At this party, present a receipt of any purchase amount at our sale and you'll get a free glass of cocktail! What are you waiting for? Join us for the fun and the drink by getting your house a nice piece of furniture at unbelievable prices.

請在11月14日晚上參加結束特賣烤肉聚會和現場演唱會。在派對上，只要您秀出一張在本拍賣購物的收據（金額不限），就可以拿到一杯免費的雞尾酒。還在等什麼？以無法置信的超低價為您的家增添一組好家具，並加入我們好好玩樂和喝一杯。

活動需攜帶的物品

◉ In appreciation of your regular patronage we wish to extend to you a personal invitation to attend a private sales of women's clothing at our department store on Friday, July 23rd starting 5:00 pm. Our regular patrons will have first selection on that day before the sale is open to the public. If you care to avail yourself of this special occasion, please bring this invitation letter with you and present it at our women's department.

為了感謝您常常光顧，我們寄出私人的邀請，歡迎您蒞臨7月23日下午五點開始，針對女裝部門辦的會員日封館特賣會。我們的常客可以在對一般大眾開放之前，優先挑選館內的服飾。如果您願意參與會員封館特賣，當天請攜帶本邀請函至女裝部門。

其他宣布活動訊息的萬用語

◉ We enclose advance announcement of our Courtesy Day of Men's Suits and Shoes.

我們附上活動通知函，優先通知您有關男裝和男鞋部門的會員特賣會訊息。

◉ As one of our regular patrons, we're informing you with delight of the up-coming anniversary sale.

您身為我們的常客，我們很高興通知您即將舉辦的週年特賣訊息。

句型解說在這裡

句型1

S + 助動詞 (can / should / may / must) + VR

否定副詞+主要子句　以倒裝句型呈現

常見否定副詞：never, nor, neither, not only, not until; (部分否定) rarely, hardly, barely, scarcely, seldom
(表示少量) little, few, only
倒裝句型：類似問句句型，Be動詞或助動詞提到主詞之前

☞ Nowhere else in town will you find better deals on the greatest furniture.
= You will not find better deals anywhere in town….
你不會在城裡其他地方以更好的價格買到最棒的家具。

延伸句型

Never + 倒裝句　　從未；決不

☞ Never will I forgive him.
= I will never forgive him. 我決不會原諒他。

Not until……+ 倒裝句　　一直到……才……

☞ Not until one loses health will he realize the importance of it.
= He won't realize the importance of health until he loses it.
要等到失去健康，才知道健康的重要。

Only……+ 倒裝句　　只有

☞ Only when you lose health do you know the importance of it.
= You know the importance of health only when you lose it.
只有當失去健康，才知其重要性。

句型2

come + (and) VR　　快來做……

☞ Come (and) visit our new apartment. 快來參觀我們的新公寓。

延伸句型

go + (and) VR　　去做……

☞ Let's go (and) see the movie. 我們一起去看電影。

比較句型

go + V-ing　　娛樂或運動

☞ She goes shopping almost every weekend.
她幾乎每週末去逛街購物。

練習時間試試看

發佈活動訊息

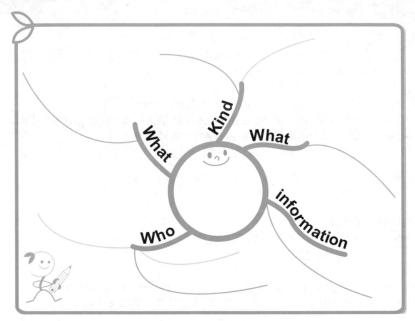

 Who are you writing to?　對象

 What is this email for?　主旨

 What is the event?　活動

 Information of the event　資訊

練習範例分享

To Ms. Tsai,

Please join Amazon for a press conference held on

Thursday, September 6, 2012 at 10:00 am at Ritz Taipei.

Amazon has unleashed new versions of our electronic

book readers as well as revealed our first multimedia

tablet. As the world's largest Internet store, we will

update our Kindle and Kindle Fire lineups. Get ready to

be impressed with the terrific features at the conference.

Get the first-hand information of our new lineup of e-book

readers, tablets and have a glimpse of our long-awaited

smartphone!

Please reply this email to confirm participation to this

press conference, so I can secure a seat for you. Feel

free to contact me for further information and request for

press packets.

Sincerely yours,

Owen Swisher

對象

主旨　活動

資訊

新品發表

蔡小姐您好：

歡迎您參加亞馬遜的記者會，時間是9月6日週四上午十點，地點在台北麗池酒店。

亞馬遜已經推出最新版的電子書，並且發表了我們第一款多媒體平板電腦。身為全世界最大網路商店，我們會更新我們的Kindle 和Kindle Fire系列商品，在記者發表會上您可以準備好見證其優越性能。

快來取得第一手我們最新電子書、平板電腦和萬眾期盼的智慧型手機情報。
請回覆此信確認參加記者會，以便為您保留座位。歡迎與我聯繫取得更多資訊或取得媒體用說明手冊。

Owen Swisher 敬上

情境二　舉辦餐會

心智圖解說

寫作技巧錦囊

Who are you writing to?　對象
→ Ms. Witty Kao

What is this email for?　主旨
→ ask attendees about their preferences, expectations of a dinner party

Questions to ask the attendee　問題
→information, menu, dress, settings, RSVP

單字片語搶先看

1. **series** *n.[C]* 系列
   * The company has just held a series of events to promote its latest products.
   這間公司剛舉辦過一連串的活動推廣最新商品。

2. **opening ceremony** 開幕典禮 (閉幕典禮：closing ceremony)
   * The mayor is invited cutting the ribbon at the opening ceremony of a new shopping mall.
   市長受邀在一個新的購物商城的開幕典禮上剪彩。

3. **dietary** *adj.* 和飲食相關的
   * This hospital cares for its patients' particular dietary needs.
   這間醫院照顧病人的特殊飲食需求。
   詞類變化：diet *n.[C,U]* 飲食；食物

4. **restriction** *n.[C]* 限制
   * When planning meals or designing menus, it is important to enquire if the guests have any special food restrictions or allergies.
   當計畫菜餚和設計菜單時，詢問賓客有無特殊食物限制或過敏是很重要的。

   詞類變化：restrict *vt.* 限制；約束

5. **attendee** *n.[C]* 與會者
   * The PR agent is helping its client to make the dinner attendee list of its annual convention dinner.
   這位公關公司的代表正在為他的客戶年度會員晚會製作與會賓客名單。
   詞類變化：attend *vt. vi.* 參加

6. **vegetarian** *n.[C]* 素食者 （口語: vegan）
   * Get delicious healthy vegetarian recipes for pasta from the chef at Hyatt Hotel.
   快來取得君悅飯店主廚推出的好吃又健康的素食義大利麵食譜。

7. **allergy** *n.[醫]* 過敏
   * Although most food allergies cause relatively mild and minor symptoms, some food allergies can cause severe reactions, and may even be life-threatening.
   儘管大部分食物過敏導致輕微症狀，有些食物過敏會導致嚴重的反應，甚至有致命的可能。
   詞類變化：allergic *adj.* 過敏的

英文範例

【★可替換其他信件詢問方式】

舉辦餐會

To Ms. Kao, Chairperson of Taipei City Women's Club,

對象

Thank you for granting us with your presence to the

dinner party we hold on 10th of June at 8 o' clock

at Hotel Hyatt. We would like to take this chance to

主旨

display our latest apparel series to all our valued

customers at the opening ceremony and hold a dinner

party right afterwards. And we're honored to know

that all the members of Taipei City Women's Club will

attend this special occasion.

To make sure we can accommodate the needs of

all our valued guests at the dinner party, we'd like

to obtain as much information as possible about the

dietary restrictions of our attendees. Your kind reply to

the following inquiries would be highly appreciated:

★ The total number of guests (including family

members):_____adults _____children (7-12) _____

問題

問題

children(under 6)

The number of guests who require vegetarian meals:

問題

問題

The number of guests who have special food limitations

and details (e.g. don't eat beef, pork, or food allergies)

問題

Please give us your confirmation by 29th of May.

問題

Thank you again for your enthusiastic participation in the

問題

event and we are looking forward to attending to you.

Sincerely yours,

Douglas Jones

段落大意

感謝參與餐會 開場感謝對方參與餐會，再次提醒餐會時間與地點。

需確認的細節 請教對方對於座位安排，餐點內容等要求或特殊喜好。

懇請回覆 要求對方回覆確認。

信尾 客套語 + 署名。

中文翻譯

台北市婦女會主席 郭小姐您好：

謝謝您答應蒞臨我們在6月10日晚上8點在君悅飯店舉辦的晚宴。我們將藉這個場合舉辦開幕典禮，為貴賓們展示我們最新的服飾系列，並隨即開始晚宴。我們很榮幸得知所有婦女會的成員都將蒞臨這個特殊的場合。

為了確定我們能照顧到所有晚宴貴賓的需求，我們想要收集詳盡的與會者對餐點的喜好資料。若您能回覆以下詢問，我們將不勝感激。
所有參與者人數（包含家族成員）：大人＿＿名，兒童（7-12歲）＿＿名，幼兒（六歲以下）＿＿＿名
點素食餐點者人數：

特殊飲食需求的人數以及細節（例如：不吃牛肉、豬肉或食物過敏）
請您在5月29日前回覆

再次謝謝您熱情參與此盛會，期待為您服務。

Douglas Jones 敬上

換個對象寫寫看

【★其他信件詢問飲食資訊的方式】

飲食特殊需求確認

- We'd like your help to make this dinner party a successful event by providing your personal food limitations or requirements. Please feel free to notify us if you have any food allergies or limitations due to religions or health concerns, so we can provide personalized / specialized meals to accommodate your needs.

  我們需要您的協助,提供您對飲食的限制或需求,讓這個餐會成功舉辦。若您對特定食物過敏,或因為宗教或健康考量不能吃特定食物,歡迎告知我們,以便為您提供符合您需求的客製化餐點。

告知餐宴的主題或特殊活動

- Join us for the Christmas casino night, with cocktails and small plates. There will be a fancy dress competition and the best couple will be offered free special dinner for New Year's Eve at W Hotel. Participation in the competition is unofficially mandatory to help spread the spirit of Christmas.

  請加入我們參加聖誕節賭博之夜,享受雞尾酒和小菜。現場也有扮裝比賽,扮裝最棒的夫妻或情侶可以獲得W飯店的晚餐免費除夕夜。為了傳遞過聖誕的氣氛和精神,不成文規定每個人都要參加扮裝比賽。

其他邀約餐會的參考句型

- Black-tie is required. Hors d'oeuvres and Cocktails at 6:30p.m.. Dinner immediately following R.S.V.P. by October 25th.

  需著正式套裝。6點半點會先上冷盤和雞尾酒,隨即開始晚宴。請在10月25日前回覆是否出席。

- Let us take the chance to invite all our sponsors and suppliers to our company's up-coming year-end dinner party on 25th December. I, on behalf of our company, have organized a buffet banquet and lot-drawing party at our head office premises itself. We sincerely hope you enjoy the party with us all.

  讓我藉這個機會邀請所有我們公司的贊助商和合作廠商參與我們公司在12月25日舉辦的的年終晚會。我代表本公司策劃在本公司總部舉辦的自助餐和抽獎,期望您與我們一起同樂。

句型解說在這裡

句型1

> right + 地方或時間副詞 (right here / right now / right afterwards / right in front of)

- We will present a cat walk show and then a dinner party is held right afterwards
  我們會先有走秀展示，隨即立刻舉辦晚宴。
- I'm running late for a class. I'm leaving right now.
  我上課要遲到了，現在就得走。

延伸概念

> right (adj.)　正確的 (=correct)

- His answer to this question is right.
  他這一題答案是正確的。

> right (adj.)　右邊的 (左邊: left)

- Walk straight along this road for two blocks and turn right.
  延這一條路走兩個街區再右轉。

句型2

> attend to　照料；照顧；服務；服侍 (=serve, take care of)

- The waiter attends to 10 guests at the same time during the dinner hours.
  這位服務生在晚餐時段一次服務10位客人 。

延伸概念

attend vt. 參加
- The CEO himself will attend the shareholders' meeting.
  公司總經理會參加股東大會。

attendee n.[C] 與會者
- All attendees to the convention should wear identification badges.
  所有年度代表大會的與會者都要佩戴識別證。

練習時間試試看

舉辦餐會

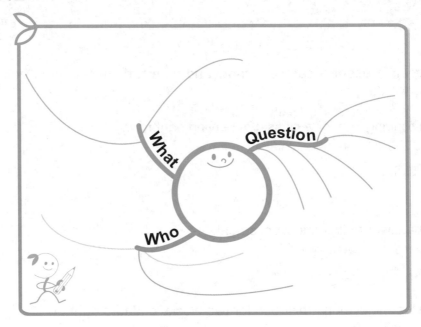

 Who are you writing to?　對象

 What is this email for?　主旨

 Questions to ask the attendees　問題

練習範例分享

To Mr. and Mrs. Paul Louis,

On behalf of Taipei Lions Club, I'd like to express our 對象

sincere gratitude to your presence in our up-coming

Sponsor Night on March 23rd at 6:30 pm at our Lions

Hall for an evening full of great food, fellowship and

valuable information about Lions Club provided by our

respected guest speaker, Mr. Vincent Wang.

To make sure we can attend to all our valued guests at 主旨

the dinner, we"d like if you have any food requirements

or allergies, so we can care for your dietary needs while 問題

you enjoy the good food, fun and some enlightenments

on how you can serve your surrounding communities

as well as around the world.

Please reply this email by March 10th as to the above

inquiries.

Thank you again for your enthusiastic participation in

the event and we look forward to meeting you.

Sincerely,

Jill Manning

Paul Louis先生、夫人好：

本人謹代表台北獅子會，感謝二位蒞臨即將在3月23日舉辦的贊助之夜，晚會時間6點半開始，地址在獅子會大樓，誠邀兩位共享一整晚的美食饗宴，聯誼，以及特別力邀貴賓Vincent Wang先生致詞，介紹獅子會相關資訊。

為了迎合所有晚宴貴賓的需求，我們想知道你們是否有任何飲食上的要求或食物過敏，好讓我們能照顧到你們的飲食需求，讓二位盡情享用美食，同樂，以及得到啟發，瞭解如何貢獻所屬社區和全世界。

請二位在3月10日前回覆郵件回答上述問題。

再次謝謝二位熱情參與此盛會，期待與你們見面。

Jill Manning敬上

情境三　填寫回函

心智圖解說

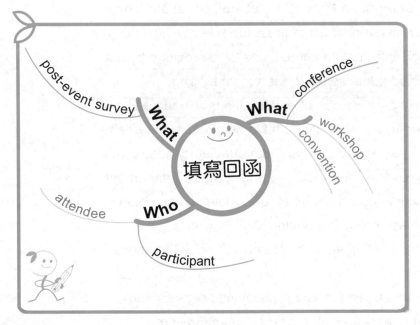

寫作技巧錦囊

Who are you writing to?　對象
→ Participant

What is the mail about?　主旨
→ post-event survey

What is the event?　活動
→ a conference / seminar / speech

單字片語搶先看

1. **conference** *n.[C]* 會議；討論會
   ☞ Representatives from over 100 countries attended the International Peace Conference.
   超過一百多國的代表參加這場國際和平會議。

2. **evaluation** *n.[C,U]* 評鑑；考核
   ☞ They took some samples of products for evaluation.
   他們從產品中取樣作檢核。
   詞類變化：evaluate vt. 估……價

3. **feedback** *n.[U]* 回饋 *(+on)*
   ☞ The teacher gave each student some feedback on their assignments.
   老師針對作業給予個別學生他的建議。

4. **collaboration** *n.[U]* 合作 *(= cooperation)*
   ☞ You can get the best deal at our anniversary sale.
   您可以在我們週年慶上獲得最超值划算的交易。

5. **relevance** *n.[U]* 相關聯性
   ☞ The university offers postgraduate programs for professionals with relevance to brand marketing.
   這所大學提供和品牌行銷相關的碩士課程。
   詞類變化：relevant adj.有相關性的；irrelevant adj.沒有相關性的

6. **forum** *n.[C]* 討論場所；交流平台 *(=platform)*
   ☞ The journal aims to provide a forum for discussion and debate.
   這個媒體雜誌目標為提供一個討論和辯論的交流平台。

7. **presentation** *n.[C,U]* 授予；介紹
   ☞ We will make a presentation to help the client fully understand our product.
   我們即將做簡報讓客戶瞭解我們的產品。
   詞類變化：present vt. 贈送

8. **confidential** *adj.* 機密的
   ☞ Doctors are required to keep patients' records completely confidential.
   醫生們被要求要將病患的病例資料完全保密。

英文範例

【★可加入其他詢問細節】

對象：參與者

Dear Participant,
We would like to thank you for your participation in the conference.

The organizing committee would like to invite you to take a moment to complete our conference evaluation feedback. Your feedback will enable us to improve our conferences and better meet your needs.
This evaluation will take no more than 5 minutes of your time.
Thanks for your collaboration.

★ 1. Please indicate your overall satisfaction with this conference:
   ☐ Very satisfied ☐ Somewhat Satisfied
   ☐ Neither satisfied nor dissatisfied
   ☐ Somewhat Dissatisfied   ☐ Very Dissatisfied
2. How would you rate the following items? (excellent / very good / good / Fair / Poor)
   ＊Relevance of conference contents
   ＊Providing a forum for exchange of information with other participants
   ＊Quality of presentations
3. What is the most valuable of the conference or any suggestions?

We highly appreciate any of your comments, ideas, and suggestions. The email will be solely for the use of evaluating this event and the information you share will be confidential.
Sincerely,
Coast Organizing Committee

段落大意

寫信目的　開場說明自己參加特定活動，提供會後感想。

感想與意見　具體說明對活動各方面的感想。

懇請回覆　感謝對方此活動，希望自己的意見能有所幫助。

信尾　客套語 + 署名。

中文翻譯

與會者您好：

我們很感謝您參與本次會議！主辦單位想要請您花一些時間完成我們會議評鑑回饋表。您的回饋能讓我們會議越辦越好，且更能符合您的需求。

這份意見表不會花您超過5分鐘的時間。謝謝您的合作。

1.請給予整體滿意度的評分：（很滿意 / 還算滿意 / 持平 / 些微不滿意 / 非常不滿意）

2.請針對以下項目評分（傑出 / 很好 / 好 / 普通 / 不佳）
　　＊會議內容的相關性
　　＊提供和其他與會者交流的平台
　　＊簡報的品質

3.本次會議最有價值之處或您的建議。
　　我們很感謝您任何的評語、想法和建議。這封郵件將純粹用來評鑑本次活動品質，您所提供的資料將被保密。

Coast主辦單位敬上

換個對象寫寫看

會議內容

- We'd like you to provide any comments or suggestions on the following criteria:
  * How useful was this conference?
  * The content was relevant / informative: The content was as advertised / what I expected
  * How do you rate the suitability of the program?
  * Do you think the registration process was smooth and efficient?
  * What do you think about the quality of material circulated / distributed / given by the organizers?
  * Were you satisfied with the organizational arrangements for and during the event?
  * What do you think about the length of the sessions?

  我們想請您針對以下項目提供您寶貴的意見和建議：
  這場討論會對您是否有用處？
  內容是否有相關性／紮實／如同廣告所描述的一樣／如同我原先預期
  提供的課程合適性如何？
  報名和簽到程序是否流暢和有效率？
  您認為主辦單位提供的資料品質如何？
  您對主辦單位行程的安排滿意嗎？
  您對於會議時間長度的想法？

- 您認為我們提供的餐點品質如何？
  您認為會議舉辦場地和設備如何？
  您認為會議舉辦日期和時間滿意嗎？
  您認為會場的交通和位置如何（會場的合適度）？

其他詢問活動意見的問題

- We'd like to invite you to fill in the satisfaction questionnaires.
  我們想請您配合填寫活動滿意度調查問卷。
- Would you recommend this event to others? (Definitely / Not Sure / May not consider)
  您會推薦這個活動給其他人嗎？（一定會／不確定／可能不考慮）
- Do you intend to attend next year's event? (Likely / Neutral / Unlikely)
  你有意願想參加明年的會議嗎？（可能／持平／不太可能）

句型解說在這裡

句型1

A enable B + to V A讓B能夠去做……

☞ The loan enabled Jan to buy the house.
這筆貸款讓Jan可以買房子。

延伸句型

be able to V　有能力去做

☞ Jan is able to buy a house with the loan.
因為有貸款，Jan能夠買房子。

have the ability to V　有能力去做

☞ Jan has the ability to buy a house because she has got the loan.
因為取得貸款，Jan有能力買房子。

–able (adj.) 複合形容詞以 "-able" 結尾，代表「可以……的」
washable (=it can be washed) 可洗的
unbreakable (=it cannot be broken) 摔不破的
loveable (=easy to love) 可愛的

句型2

事物 + take + sb. + 時間 + to V(不加受詞)　事物花某人……時間去……

☞ This feedback form took me a minute to complete.
這份意見表花了我一分鐘時間完成。

延伸句型

It takes / took sb. + 時間 + to V(含受詞)

☞ It took me a minute to complete this feedback form.

比較句型

sb. + spend / spent + 時間 + on N / (in) Ving

☞ I spent a minute completing the feedback form.
=I spent a minute on the feedback form.

練習時間試試看

填寫回函

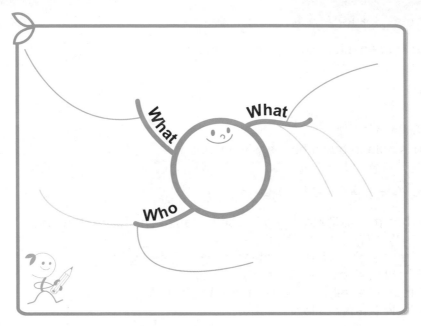

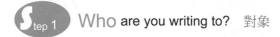

Step 1　Who are you writing to?　對象

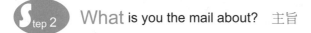

Step 2　What is you the mail about?　主旨

Step 3　What is the event?　活動

練習範例分享

Dear Participants,

We would like to thank you for your participation in the ——— 對象

Fresh Career Workshop, which was aimed to prepare you ——— 主旨

for job interviews. ——— 活動

We'd like you to take a moment to complete our feedback ——— 主旨

survey, so we can improve the series of workshops.

Thanks for your cooperation.

1. Please rate the following items by 1-5, 5 being the highest score:

Instructor Effectiveness:

The instructor has prepared well for the lesson.

The instructor is able to explain the points clearly.

The instructor is able to hold my interest.

The instructor interacts well with the class.

2. What do you think were the strengths of this course?

3. What could we do better?

We highly appreciate any of your comments, ideas, and suggestions. Thank you again for your participating in the event.

Sincerely,

Julie Brooms

Organizer of the workshop

與會者您好：

我們很感謝您參與本次職涯開展講座，此會議目的是讓您能準備工作的面試。我們想請您花一些時間完成我們回饋意見調查表，您的回饋能讓我們這系列的講座越辦越好。謝謝您的合作。

1. 請針對以下項目以數字1到5評分（5為最高分）

   演講者的內容：

   演講者充分準備演講內容

   演講者將內容要點解釋清楚

   演講者讓我保持興趣和專注

   演講者和全班互動良好

2. 本次講座成功之處：

3. 我們可以改進之處：

我們很感謝您任何的評語、想法和建議。再次謝謝您的參與本活動。

主辦人Julie Brooms敬上

心智圖學 E-mail 寫作好 easy

作者	陳瑾珮
發行人	周瑞德
企畫編輯	倍斯特編輯部
圖片來源	www.dreamstime.com
封面設計	King Chen
內頁構成	好映像有限公司
印製	世和印製企業有限公司
初版	2013 年 5 月
定價	新台幣 349 元
出版	倍斯特出版事業有限公司
電話	（02）2351-2007
傳真	（02）2351-0887
地址	10078 台北市中正區福州街 1 號 10 樓之 2
Email	best.books.service@gmail.com
總經銷	商流文化事業有限公司
地址	235 新北市中和區中正路 752 號 8 樓
電話	（02）2228-8841
傳真	（02）2228-6939

國家圖書管出版品預行編目（CIP）資料

心智圖學 E-mail 寫作好 easy / 陳瑾珮著 .
-- 初版 . -- 臺北市：倍斯特 , 2013. 5
面；　公分
ISBN：978-986-88732-1-6(平裝)
1. 英語 2. 電子郵件 3. 應用文
805.179　　　　　　　　　　　　101018885